OCEAN CITY SEA GLASS

CLAUDIA VANCE

CHAPTER ONE

The boat ramp at Tennessee Avenue was quiet at seven in the morning. A couple of fishermen were loading their gear, and a woman walked her golden retriever along the water's edge. Lauren adjusted the straps of her life jacket and looked out at the bay, calm and glassy in the early light.

"Perfect conditions," Matt said as he pulled their two kayaks from the back of his Jeep. "Low tide, no wind. We picked a good morning."

"We did," Lauren said.

Matt set the paddles beside the kayaks.

Lauren walked toward the shoreline, her sneakers crunching on exposed shells. She could see patches of seagrass and clusters of barnacle-covered rocks that would be underwater in a few hours.

"We've got about four hours before the tide starts coming back in," Matt said, checking his watch as they carried the first kayak down to the water. "Plenty of time to explore."

"Then let's make the most of it." Lauren climbed into her kayak and pushed off, the paddle slicing through the shallow water. Within seconds, Matt was beside her, his strokes steady and practiced.

The June morning had started gray, with a thick marine layer sitting over Ocean City like a blanket. It gave everything a muted, almost dreamlike quality.

A family of sandpipers worked their way along the mudflat, their thin legs moving in quick bursts as they probed for breakfast. Lauren watched them for a moment, charmed by their single-minded focus.

"Which way do you want to head?" Matt asked, his paddle resting across his lap as he drifted alongside.

Lauren pointed south. "Let's go past the jetty. I've always wondered what's on the other side."

"The mysterious south end," Matt said with mock drama. "I've been down there a few times, but never by kayak. Usually the current's too strong near the rocks."

"Low tide should help with that," Lauren said. "Less water means less current, right?"

Matt considered this. "In theory. Let's find out."

They paddled without talking for a while, the only sounds the gentle splash of their paddles and the occasional cry of a gull overhead. Lauren loved mornings like this with Matt, when they could just exist together without the demands of their businesses pulling them in different directions. Days off together were rare once summer started.

She thought about the past few weeks, the flurry of activity as she'd prepared both businesses for the summer rush. Romano's had exceeded all her expectations, and Chipper's was as busy as ever, the breakfast crowds lining up before they even opened the doors.

"You're doing that thing again," Matt said, glancing over at her.

"What thing?"

"Where you're physically here but mentally back at the restaurant, making a checklist in your head."

Lauren laughed because it was true. She'd been thinking about whether Bobby had remembered to order more eggs and whether the new server she'd hired was going to work out. "Sorry. Old habits."

"No apology needed. Just wanted to remind you that we're out here to enjoy ourselves. The restaurant will survive without you for a few hours."

They rounded the curve of the shoreline, and the jetty came into view. It stretched out into the ocean like a rocky finger, black boulders piled high to create a barrier against the relentless waves. Lauren had seen it from the beach many times but had never paddled this close. With the tide so low, the rocks extended even farther than usual, creating a maze of partially exposed boulders.

"Hold on," Matt said, stopping his paddle mid-stroke. "Do you see that?"

Lauren followed his gaze. Just beyond the jetty, where the rocks curved back toward the shore, there appeared to be an opening. A gap in the boulder line that she'd never noticed before.

"Should we check it out?"

Matt was already paddling toward it. "Absolutely."

As they approached, Lauren saw that the gap opened into a narrow channel between the rocks. Where it led, she couldn't tell.

"This is incredible," Lauren said as they entered the channel. The rocks rose up on either side of them, worn smooth by decades of ocean water. Strands of kelp draped over the lower boulders like green curtains, and tiny crabs scuttled into crevices as they passed.

The channel curved to the left then split into two passages. Matt pointed to the wider one on the right, and they paddled through, only to find it dead-ended against a wall of encrusted rock.

"Back up," Matt said, and they reversed course, taking the narrower passage instead.

This one twisted sharply, the rocks pressing close. Lauren

had to duck under a low overhang of stone hung with seaweed. For a moment, she couldn't see anything ahead but more rock, and she wondered if they'd made a mistake coming in here.

"You okay?" Matt called from behind her.

"I think so. It's tight."

It curved again, and Lauren lost her sense of direction. Were they heading toward the ocean or back toward the bay? The gray sky above gave no clues, and the rocks blocked any view of the shore. She was about to suggest they turn around when the channel suddenly widened.

"There's another split," she said.

Matt pulled up next to her. Three passages branched off in different directions, all of them narrow, all of them disappearing around blind corners.

"Left feels right," Matt said. "I think I can hear waves."

Lauren listened. Sure enough, somewhere ahead, she could hear the faint rush and retreat of the ocean.

They took the left passage, which snaked through two more sharp turns before the water became too shallow to paddle. Lauren's kayak scraped against the sandy bottom.

"End of the line for these," Matt said, climbing out into ankle-deep water. He pulled his kayak up onto a flat rock and helped Lauren do the same.

"We can walk the rest," Lauren said, peering ahead. The passage continued, but the water had drained to just a few inches, trickling over sand and shells.

They continued on foot, stepping carefully over slippery rocks and through tide pools. One final turn, and then it opened up into a hidden cove that made Lauren catch her breath.

It spread out before them, a sheltered pocket of shoreline with rock formations flanking the entrance on either side. The far end opened to the ocean, but the angle of the rocks would protect it from the main current. A crescent of sandy beach curved along the inner edge, and beyond that, the land rose gently into a stretch of dunes covered in beach grass, bayberry shrubs, and stunted pines. It looked almost like a small abandoned island, cut off from the rest of Ocean City by the maze of rocks they'd just navigated.

A single piece of driftwood, bleached white by sun and salt, lay across the highest point of the shore.

But it wasn't the shape of the cove that stopped Lauren cold. It was what covered every inch of the beach.

Sea glass. Everywhere.

Not scattered pieces here and there, the way you'd find on any Ocean City beach if you looked hard enough. This was something else entirely. The entire stretch was carpeted in it, layers upon layers of tumbled glass in every color imaginable, so dense that she couldn't see the sand beneath.

"Matt," Lauren whispered, as if speaking too loudly might break whatever spell had created this place. "Are you seeing what I'm seeing?"

Matt stopped at her side, his mouth hanging open. "This can't be real."

Lauren stepped forward and crouched at the shoreline, sifting through the glass. She lifted one from the pile, larger than any she'd ever seen, a deep blue that seemed to glow even in the soft morning light. The surface was perfectly frosted, not a single sharp edge anywhere, polished by years of tumbling in the surf.

"This is cobalt blue," Lauren said, turning it over in her hands. "Do you know how rare this is? I read that you might find one piece this color for every two or three hundred pieces of sea glass. And they're usually tiny."

"How do you know this?" Matt asked.

"A woman at Romano's told me to watch for sea glass this summer," Lauren said, still staring at the cobalt piece. "Something about the nor'easters churning things up. I didn't really believe her, but I did some reading anyway."

Matt knelt a few feet away, running his hands through the

glass. "There's red in here. Actual red sea glass. And orange." He held up a piece that looked like frozen sunset, a deep amber that faded to orange at the edges.

Lauren moved deeper onto the beach, each step producing a gentle clinking sound as the glass shifted beneath her feet. She spotted purple pieces mixed with the more common greens and browns, yellows that ranged from pale lemon to deep gold, and more blue than she could have imagined. There were thick chunks from old medicine bottles, thin curved pieces from drinking glasses, and slabs so heavy they must have come from ship windows or industrial containers.

"How is this possible?" she asked. "Sea glass takes fifty years or more to get this frosted. And the colors..." She shook her head, trying to comprehend what she was looking at. "Red glass was never common—too expensive to produce. And cobalt-blue bottles mostly disappeared after the 1950s when everything switched to plastic. This collection could span a hundred years."

Matt looked up at her. "You really did your research."

"When something piques my interest, I go down a rabbit hole," Lauren said. "I didn't expect to actually use any of it."

Matt stood up and surveyed the cove, studying the rock formations. "The way these rocks are positioned, anything that washed in here would get trapped. The ocean current would tumble the glass against the rocks over and over, but the pieces couldn't escape." He turned to look back at the passage they'd come through. "But that channel we paddled through—did you notice the bottom? It was mostly sand, not rock."

She thought back—the passage floor had been sandy, unlike the rocky walls.

"I think this cove was cut off," Matt said slowly, working through the idea. "Completely inaccessible. You can't get in from the ocean side—too many rocks, too shallow. And the bay side was blocked until the nor'easters this winter shifted enough sand to connect that sandbar. Created a passage where there wasn't one before."

"That's why nobody's ever found this place," Lauren said. "It wasn't just hidden. It was unreachable."

She walked to where the waves met the shore. As she watched, each wave deposited glass onto the beach.

"It's still coming," she said, amazed. "The source is still active somewhere out there."

Matt joined her, watching as another wave delivered more glass. "There must be something offshore," he said. "Something feeding this."

She pulled out her phone and snapped a few pictures of the cove and the glass scattered across the beach.

They spent the next hour exploring the cove.

Near the rocks, Lauren discovered a section where the glass had accumulated nearly a foot deep. When she dug her fingers in, she found that the pieces on the bottom were even more frosted than those on top, suggesting they'd been there longer, perhaps much longer.

"Come look at this," she called to Matt, who was examining something closer to the waves.

He made his way over, and she showed him the depth of the accumulation. "It's like geological layers," she said. "The oldest pieces at the bottom, newest on top. This has been building up for decades, maybe longer."

Matt sat back on his heels. "And the tide keeps adding to it. This could be one of the most significant sea glass deposits on the entire East Coast."

"I think you might be right," Lauren said, carefully smoothing the glass back over the spot she'd disturbed. She glanced at her watch. "We should go. Once the tide comes in, that overhang will be underwater, and the current through the channel will be a lot stronger."

They retraced their steps through the passage, picking their way over wet stone and around shallow pools. When they reached the kayaks, Lauren noticed the water had already risen a few inches.

"Good timing," Matt said, pushing his kayak off the rock and into the water.

They paddled back through the twisting channel, which already seemed slightly different than before. The water was definitely rising, covering rocks that had been exposed earlier. Lauren took one last look over her shoulder at the passage before they rounded the curve and it disappeared from view.

The return trip felt different than the journey out. Lauren's mind was racing, trying to process what they'd discovered.

The marine layer was starting to lift as they paddled, patches of blue sky appearing overhead. By noon, the gray would burn off entirely and Ocean City would be bathed in summer sunshine. Families would fill the beaches, kids would run screaming into the waves, and the boardwalk would come alive with the sounds and smells of summer vacation.

None of them would have any idea what lay hidden just beyond the jetty.

CHAPTER TWO

On the other side of Ocean City, Nancy sat at her dining room table, staring at the array of equipment spread out before her. A microphone on a small stand. A pair of headphones. Her laptop, open to a recording program she didn't fully understand. And Joe, hunched over his phone, watching what appeared to be his fourteenth YouTube tutorial on podcast production.

"Okay, I think I've got it," Joe said, though he sounded anything but confident. "The levels need to stay in the green zone. If they go into the red, we're peaking."

Nancy nodded. She'd done some reading of her own, but her research had focused more on interview techniques than technical specifications.

The whole thing had started as a passing comment at a dinner with friends. Nancy had been telling stories about the old Ocean City she remembered from years past, the characters who used to run the boardwalk shops. Her friend Kelly had said, "You should record these. Before all those people are gone and the memories go with them."

The idea had taken root and refused to let go.

"I think we're ready," Nancy said, though ready was the last thing she felt. Her first interview was scheduled to start soon. Jean Vogel, ninety-two years old, had lived in Ocean City since 1951. She'd run a candy shop on the boardwalk for forty years before retiring, and she was rumored to have stories about everyone who'd ever mattered in town.

"What are you going to ask her?" Joe asked, finally setting down his phone.

"I have a list." Nancy pulled out a notebook covered in her handwriting. "I want to ask about the candy shop, obviously. But I also want to know what the boardwalk was like when she first got here. What's changed, what's stayed the same."

"That's good stuff." Joe nodded approvingly. "People will want to hear about that."

"If anyone listens."

"They'll listen. You're a natural storyteller, Nancy. Always have been."

She appreciated his confidence, even if she didn't fully share it. She doubted many people cared about the past the way she did. But that wasn't really the point. The stories deserved to be saved, whether ten people heard them or ten thousand.

The truth was, she had no idea what she was doing. She'd never recorded anything more complicated than a voicemail, didn't understand half the terminology in the tutorials Joe had shown her. And the idea of putting her voice out into the world, where anyone could hear it, made her stomach flip in ways she hadn't expected.

But there was also excitement underneath the nerves. All those conversations with old-timers at coffee shops and neighborhood gatherings—someone should capture them before they were lost. And if she didn't do it, who would?

"Let's do a test run," Joe suggested. "You ask me something, I'll answer, and we'll see how it sounds."

Nancy pressed the record button. "Joe Romano, you've

been coming to Ocean City since you were a kid. What's your earliest memory of this place?"

Joe leaned toward the microphone, too close, causing the levels to spike red. He pulled back and tried again. "My earliest memory? I must have been about six. My parents drove us down from Philly in this old station wagon. I remember the smell when we got close to the water. Salt and fish and something else. I thought it was the most exciting smell in the world."

Nancy smiled, forgetting they were recording. "What else do you remember?"

"The boardwalk seemed enormous. And the sounds. Music from every direction, the games, people calling out. My father bought me a slice of pizza bigger than my head." Joe's eyes had gone distant. "We stayed in a little rental apartment near the beach. My brother and I slept on the floor, and we thought it was the greatest adventure."

Nancy stopped the recording and played it back. The audio was rougher than she'd like, but their voices came through clearly.

"Jean Vogel should be here soon," Joe said, checking the clock.

"I told her we'd keep it to an hour, but everyone says once she gets talking, she doesn't stop."

"That's what you want for a podcast, isn't it?"

"I hope so." Nancy closed her notebook and stared at the microphone. "I keep thinking about all the people we should have recorded years ago. Do you remember Mr. Pacheco? He used to run the fishing pier. He knew everything about the waters around here, the history of the boats, the families who'd been fishing these shores for generations. He died in 2019, and all that knowledge went with him."

"You can't save everything, Nancy."

"I know. But maybe I can save some of it. Maybe that's enough."

Joe was setting out a plate of pastries from the Italian bakery on Asbury Avenue—Jean Vogel was known for her sweet tooth—when the doorbell rang.

Jean stood on the porch, immaculately dressed, her white hair styled in a careful wave. She carried a large handbag and a photo album.

"I brought pictures," she announced before Nancy could even say hello. "You said you wanted to talk about the old days. Well, I have evidence."

Nancy laughed and ushered her inside. "Jean, you didn't have to bring anything. I just want to hear what you remember."

"Stories are better with pictures." Jean followed Nancy to the dining room, where they'd set up the microphone on the table. She settled into one of the chairs and examined the microphone with interest. "This is the contraption, huh? Looks like something from a spaceship."

"It's simpler than it looks," Joe said, glancing at his laptop screen. "Just talk normal and it picks up everything."

"Normal. Right." Jean set her photo album on the table and opened it. "Should I wait until you tell me to start?"

Nancy took her seat across from Jean and started recording. "We're recording now. Just pretend it's a regular conversation."

"A regular conversation that strangers might hear?"

"Hopefully a few." Nancy glanced at her notes. "Let's start at the beginning. You moved to Ocean City in 1951. What brought you here?"

Jean's expression shifted, the theatrical nervousness giving way to something more genuine. "My husband, Frank. God rest his soul. He'd gotten a job at the fish processing plant that used to be near West Avenue. We'd been living with his parents in Camden, and when this opportunity came up, we jumped at it. A chance to have our own place, even if it was just a tiny apartment above a hardware store."

"What was Ocean City like back then?"

"It felt different. You knew everybody, and everybody knew your business." Jean flipped to a page in her album. "This is the boardwalk in 1953. Look at what people are wearing. The women in those fitted one-pieces with the little skirts, the men in those tiny swim trunks. And you see this blurry figure here? That's Sal Velluto. Ran the ring toss for thirty years. He could guess your weight within two pounds just by looking at you. Completely blind in one eye, too."

Nancy leaned forward to examine the photograph. The boardwalk was recognizable but transformed, like looking at an old friend who'd aged beyond recognition.

"Tell me about your candy shop," Nancy said. "How did that come about?"

Jean's face lit up. "That's a story. Frank worked at the fish plant for eight years, saved every penny we could. In 1959, there was a little storefront available on the boardwalk. Cheap, because it was in bad shape. Nobody wanted it. But Frank looked at me and said, 'Jean, what if we fixed it up and sold candy?' I thought he was crazy. But we did it anyway."

"What kind of candy?"

"Everything. Saltwater taffy, fudge, caramel apples, choco-late-covered anything you could think of. But our specialty was the saltwater taffy. We made it ourselves, right there in the back of the shop. You could watch through the window. Kids loved that." Jean turned another page, revealing a photograph of a younger version of herself standing behind a counter piled with colorful candy. "That's me in 1962. Look at that hair. I spent hours on that hair."

Nancy grinned. "You look beautiful."

"I looked exhausted. Running a candy shop in the summer is no joke. But it was good exhaustion. The kind that comes from building something."

They talked for over an hour, Jean's recollections spiraling out in unexpected directions.

"There was this one summer," Jean said, lowering her voice

like she was sharing a secret. "A man came into the shop every morning for a week. Same time, same order—dark chocolate fudge and a root beer. He was famous. A singer. I won't say who."

"You can't just leave it there," Nancy said.

"I can, and I will. But I'll tell you this—he was hiding from someone. A woman, I think. He had that look. You know the look. Like a man who'd made promises he couldn't keep."

She talked about a storm one summer that knocked out the power for three days, and everyone on the boardwalk shared what food they had before it spoiled. "We set up tables right on the boards," she said. "Strangers eating dinner together by candlelight. People still talk about that storm like it was a party."

And she talked about Frank, the way he'd sing to himself while pulling taffy, how he'd slip free samples to kids whose parents looked like they were counting pennies. "He never could turn away a sad face," Jean said. "That man gave away more candy than he sold some days. Drove me crazy. But that was Frank."

Jean closed her photo album. "Ocean City looks like a sweet beach town, and it is. But it's also got layers. Like anywhere else. Good people who did questionable things. Questionable people who did good things. Everyone's got their complications."

"That's what makes it interesting," Nancy said.

Jean smiled. "That's what makes it human."

Joe stopped the recording and announced that they'd captured over ninety minutes of material. Jean seemed pleased with herself, accepting a pastry and a cup of coffee before gathering her things to leave.

"You'll let me know when this goes up on the computer?" she asked at the door.

"Absolutely. We'll send you a link."

"Good. I want to hear how I sound. And I want to make sure you didn't make me look foolish."

"Impossible," Nancy assured her. "You were wonderful."

After Jean left, Nancy and Joe sat together, listening to portions of the recording. The audio quality was better than their test runs, and Jean's voice came through strong and clear. Her stories were funny and poignant and occasionally surprising in ways Nancy hadn't anticipated.

"This is good," Joe said. "Better than I expected."

"It needs editing. Some parts drag, and there's that section where the phone rang and we had to pause."

Joe leaned back in his chair. "You did great, Nancy. You asked good questions. You let her talk without interrupting. You've got a knack for this."

"I was terrified the whole time."

"It didn't show."

Nancy opened her notebook again. "There's someone I'm excited to talk to next—I've heard some interesting things about them." She looked out the window at the gray sky. "I've got dozens of names in here. More than we could ever get to. But we'll start with what we can manage. One story at a time."

"One story at a time," Joe agreed.

They spent the rest of the afternoon reviewing the recording and making notes about which sections to keep and which to trim. Nancy found herself already thinking about her next interview, the questions she'd ask, the threads she wanted to follow. Jean had been right about one thing: Ocean City had depth. And Nancy had only just started to explore it.

* * *

Claire stood in front of her bathroom mirror, trying to decide if the blouse she'd chosen was too much. Or not enough. She honestly couldn't remember what people wore on first dates anymore. The last time she'd been on a first date, most people still had flip phones and Instagram didn't exist yet.

"This is ridiculous," she said to her reflection. The reflection looked back at her, neither agreeing nor disagreeing.

The house felt strange without Evan and Bridget. They'd left for Pennsylvania three days ago to spend two weeks with their dad, Brian. Claire had spent the first two days catching up on work and reorganizing closets. By the third day, the silence had started to feel oppressive rather than peaceful.

Was it too soon for this? She and Brian had only been separated for two months. The lawyers were still going back and forth on custody details, and they had another sixty days before the divorce would be finalized. Part of her felt like she should be home in sweatpants, processing her feelings, maybe journaling or crying into a pint of ice cream like they did in the movies.

But then she thought about Melissa.

Brian had called last week, ostensibly to discuss the kids' summer schedule, and had worked in the information that he and Melissa were "getting more serious." Three years he'd known that woman. Three years of working in the same department, grabbing coffee, building something Claire hadn't even known existed. He swore nothing happened until after she'd moved to Ocean City, but did it matter? He'd moved on. He had someone waiting in the wings the whole time, whether he admitted it or not.

So when she'd found herself downloading a dating app at eleven o'clock on a Tuesday night, she'd surprised herself by actually filling out a profile. What was the harm in dipping a toe in the dating pool? She wasn't looking for anything serious. Just someone to have dinner with, maybe remind her what it felt like to be Claire again.

Glen had messaged her the next morning. His profile said he was in logistics, recently divorced, and looking for "real connection." They'd exchanged a few messages, he'd suggested dinner, and before she could overthink it, she'd said yes.

She'd chosen a seafood restaurant in Somers Point, just off the island. Neutral territory. Somewhere she could make a quick exit if things went sideways.

Claire smoothed down her blouse one more time, grabbed her purse, and headed out the door before she could change her mind.

* * *

The restaurant had a view of the water and white tablecloths, the kind of place that looked nice enough in the photos online. Claire arrived five minutes early and ordered a glass of white wine while she waited.

At exactly seven o'clock, a man walked through the door, spotted her, and made his way over. He was average height, with graying hair, and he wore a freshly pressed button-down shirt. At least he matched his profile pictures.

"Claire?" he asked, extending his hand. "Glen. Finally. You would not believe the drive I just had."

"Traffic?" Claire asked, shaking his hand.

"Traffic, construction, some guy in a Prius going forty in the left lane." Glen sat down heavily and immediately started looking around for the server. "And the GPS took me on this ridiculous route through Margate. Added twenty minutes. I'm going to leave a bad review."

"For the GPS?"

"For Google Maps. They need to know." He finally flagged down a server, a young woman who approached with a polite smile. "Bourbon, neat. What do you have that's top shelf?"

The server listed three options.

"That's it? Fine, the Blanton's." He waved his hand. "Actually, wait. Is it cold? The bourbon. Sometimes restaurants refrigerate it, which is completely wrong."

"It's room temperature, sir."

"Fine. Blanton's." Glen turned back to Claire as the server escaped. "You have to ask these things. I once got a bourbon that was practically ice cold. Sent it back twice."

Claire took a sip of her wine.

"So, this place," Glen said, looking around with obvious disapproval. "I read the reviews, and they were mostly positive, but already I'm not impressed. That music—" He gestured toward the speakers, which were playing soft jazz. "Who wants to listen to jazz at dinner? It's so pretentious."

"I kind of like jazz."

"Really?" Glen looked at her like she'd admitted to enjoying dental work. "Anyway, I had a crazy week. Work has been insane. Did I mention what I do? I'm in logistics. Supply chain optimization. It's incredibly complex—nobody really understands it when I explain it, but basically I'm the guy who makes sure everything runs smoothly. Companies would fall apart without people like me."

Claire opened her mouth to respond, but Glen was already continuing.

"I've been with my company for twelve years. Started in the warehouse, if you can believe it. Now I manage a team of fifteen. Could be more, but I turned down a promotion last year. The hours weren't worth it. I already work fifty, sixty hours a week. My ex-wife used to complain about it constantly. 'You're never home, Glen. You missed the kids' recital, Glen.' As if I could just leave in the middle of a supply chain crisis."

The server returned with Glen's bourbon. He took a sip and immediately grimaced.

"This isn't Blanton's."

"It is, sir. I poured it myself."

"It doesn't taste like Blanton's. It tastes like—" He took another sip, making a show of swirling it in his mouth. "Fine. Whatever. It's fine."

She set down menus and retreated quickly.

"Where was I?" Glen said. "Right, my ex. The divorce was brutal. She got the house, half my 401k, and I'm paying alimony for another three years. Three years! For a ten-year marriage. The system is completely rigged against men." Glen took a long drink of his bourbon—the bourbon he'd just complained about—and signaled for another. "But honestly? Best thing that ever happened to me. I've got my freedom now. I can do whatever I want."

Claire glanced at her wine glass, calculating how quickly she could finish it.

"I've been really getting into self-improvement lately," Glen continued. "Biohacking, optimization, that kind of thing. Do you know what biohacking is?"

"I've heard of—"

"It's basically taking control of your own biology. I do cold plunges every morning. Three minutes in forty-degree water. Not everyone can handle it, but I've trained myself. Mind over matter." He tapped his temple. "I've also got this morning routine. Takes two hours, but it's worth it. I wake up at four-thirty, meditate, journal, work out. There's actually research that shows—"

The young woman approached to take their food orders. Claire ordered the salmon, grateful for the interruption.

"I'll do the filet," Glen said. "Medium rare. Actually, what's the temperature on that? Can you ask the chef to cook it to exactly one hundred thirty degrees internal? And make sure it's grass-finished, not just grass-fed. There's a huge difference. Also, is the butter clarified or regular? I can't do regular butter. Inflammation."

She wrote something down and practically fled.

"You have to advocate for yourself in restaurants," Glen explained. "Otherwise they just give you whatever. So, do you have kids?"

"Two. Evan is ten, Bridget is twelve. They're with their dad right now."

"Smart. Shared custody." Glen nodded approvingly. "I see my kids every other weekend. Works out great. They're teenagers now, so half the time they just want to sit on their phones anyway. We'll be closer when they're adults."

Claire doubted that very much.

Their entrees arrived. Claire's salmon looked fine. Glen immediately cut into his steak and frowned, but said nothing. Small mercies.

She ate half her salmon before giving up. Her appetite had disappeared somewhere around the cold-plunge conversation.

She looked at her watch. She'd been here for an hour and twelve minutes. It felt like a lifetime.

"You're quiet," Glen observed, as if noticing her for the first time all evening. "I like that. Most people just want to talk about themselves, you know?"

Claire almost laughed.

"I think I should probably head out."

"Already?" Glen looked surprised. "I was going to suggest dessert. They have a chocolate lava cake here that's supposed to be decent, though I doubt it lives up to the hype. Nothing ever does."

"I have an early morning."

"Fair enough." Glen signaled for the check. "So, this was fun. We should do it again."

Claire stood up and pulled out cash for her portion of the bill. "It was nice meeting you, Glen."

"I'll text you," Glen said. "Maybe we can do this weekend? I'm free Saturday after my workout and my chiropractor appointment. I've got this thing with my L4 vertebra. Very complicated. I could tell you about it at dinner."

"I'll check my schedule."

"Great. Oh, and Claire?" Glen smiled, apparently convinced the evening had been a roaring success. "I had a really nice time. It's refreshing to meet someone who's a good listener."

Claire managed a nod and headed for the door. She didn't look back.

Outside, the evening air felt like freedom. She walked to her car, got in, and sat there for a moment with her hands on the steering wheel.

Then she started laughing.

She laughed until her eyes watered, until she had to wipe her face with a napkin from her glove compartment. Glen was going to text her about a second date. Glen genuinely thought he was a good conversationalist. Glen's ex-wife was probably somewhere right now, enjoying a quiet dinner without hearing about cold plunges or morning routines, and Claire hoped that woman knew how lucky she was.

She pulled out her phone and stared at the dating app icon. She could delete it. Go back to her quiet evenings and stop subjecting herself to this.

But no. She closed the app and dropped her phone back in her purse. She'd try again. Not tonight, but eventually.

Tonight, she was going home to take a bath and watch something mindless on television. She'd earned it.

She started the car and headed back over the bridge to Ocean City, still smiling.

CHAPTER THREE

The call came in at seven-fifteen in the morning, just as Brenna was scanning the tide charts on her laptop.

"Ms. Groff? This is Lieutenant Morrison with the Beach Patrol. We've got a situation down at Twenty-Third Street, and someone suggested you might be the person to call."

Brenna closed her laptop. "What kind of situation?"

"Jellyfish. A lot of them. They started washing up yesterday evening, and this morning the whole beach looks like something out of a science fiction movie. I need to figure out what we're dealing with here, and someone from Parks and Rec said we should get an expert opinion."

Twenty minutes later, Brenna stood at the water's edge with her boots ankle-deep in foam, staring at a sight that made her stomach tighten with professional concern.

Moon jellyfish. Hundreds of them. Maybe thousands. They carpeted the sand in translucent heaps, their bodies pale and glassy, each one the size of a dinner plate. The distinctive four-ring pattern—purple-pink horseshoes—was visible through the dome of each bell. Some still held their shape, quivering like mounds of wet gelatin. Others had already begun to flatten and deflate in the morning sun, their edges going cloudy. The tide line was thick with them, and more kept washing in with every wave.

The morning was already starting to heat up, the sky a clear blue that promised another scorching June day. A handful of early beachgoers had gathered behind the yellow tape the Beach Patrol had strung up, pointing and taking photos with their phones. One teenager had his arm extended for a selfie with the jellyfish field in the background.

Lieutenant Morrison stood beside her, a stocky man in his fifties with the weathered complexion of someone who'd spent his career outdoors. "I've worked this beach for twenty-three years," he said. "Never seen anything like this."

"Neither have I." Brenna crouched down to examine one of the specimens more closely, careful not to touch the trailing tentacles. The jellyfish were in various states—some still pulsing faintly, clinging to the last traces of life, others clearly dead and losing their shape. "Moon jellies are common in these waters, but not in these numbers. Not all at once like this."

"So what does it mean?"

That was the question. Brenna's mind was already cycling through possibilities: water temperature changes, shifts in current patterns, disruption of their normal habitat, changes in the populations of prey species. Jellyfish blooms could be indicators of larger problems in marine ecosystems, early warning signals that something was out of balance.

She stood and walked along the tide line, counting specimens in her head, trying to get a sense of the bloom's density. Every few feet she'd kneel beside one for a closer look, noting size variations, looking for any species other than the typical moon jellies. Near the lifeguard stand, currently unmanned this early in the morning, she found a cluster of lion's mane jellyfish mixed in with the moon jellies. Their reddish-brown tentacles were far more dangerous than the moon jellies'.

"Lieutenant," she called out. "We've got lion's mane over

here too. That changes things. Your crew needs to be extra careful during cleanup."

Morrison jogged over, his face grim when he saw what she was pointing at. "Those are the bad ones, right?"

"Worse than moon jellies, definitely. Their stings are painful and can cause severe reactions in people with allergies—difficulty breathing, nausea. Anyone handling these needs full protective gear." She photographed the specimens with her phone, adding notes about location and time.

Morrison watched her work. "So what's causing all this?"

"I'm not sure yet," she admitted. "I need to collect some samples, check water temperature, see if there's anything unusual happening out in the bay." She took a few more pictures, documenting the extent of the bloom. "You should definitely keep the beach closed for now. Moon jellies aren't as dangerous as some species, but their stings can still irritate skin, especially in children or anyone who's sensitive. And with lion's mane in the mix, we can't take any chances."

Morrison nodded. "I'll get the signs going up. Parks department is sending a crew with rakes and bags once you give the go-ahead. They want to know if it's safe to handle them."

"Gloves and long sleeves, and they should be fine. The stinging cells can still fire even after the jellyfish is dead, but the venom isn't strong. More of an annoyance than a danger for most people."

She spent the next two hours working the beach, collecting samples, measuring water temperature at various points, making notes about current direction and wave patterns. The bloom extended for at least half a mile in either direction from where she'd started. By the time she finished, the sun was high overhead and sweat was trickling down her back.

A small crowd had gathered beyond the Beach Patrol barriers, summer visitors curious about the unusual closure. Brenna overheard fragments of conversation as she made her way back to her truck. Speculation about pollution, about climate change, about whether this meant the beaches would be safe to swim in tomorrow.

Her phone buzzed as she loaded the last samples into the truck. A text from her supervisor at the research station: "Heard about the jellies. Keep me posted. Might need to loop in the state marine lab."

After typing a quick response, she paused, looking back at the beach. Something was happening in the waters around Ocean City, drawing thousands of jellyfish to shore. The question was whether this was a one-time event or the start of a trend.

She checked her other messages. Nothing from Josh.

It had been almost two weeks since he'd asked her to get coffee. Two weeks of texts back and forth, each of them perpetually busy with work, schedules that never quite aligned. She'd started to wonder if the invitation had been a polite gesture rather than a genuine interest, if he'd moved on to other things while she was out counting terrapins and writing grant applications.

But that didn't feel right. There had been a warmth in the way he'd looked at her that morning at the animal hospital, a quality that had stayed with her longer than it probably should have.

She climbed into the truck and pulled out of the parking lot, headed toward the research station, her mind split between the jellyfish bloom and wondering if she should just pick up the phone and call him.

* * *

The research station was a converted boathouse on the bay side of the island, a modest building with weathered cedar shingles and a dock that extended out over the water. Brenna had spent countless hours here since March, processing samples, entering data, meeting with volunteers, but today the space felt particularly quiet. Her two graduate assistants were both in the field, and the usual background hum of activity was absent.

She set up her samples in the small laboratory space, labeling each one with the time and location of collection. The jellyfish specimens floated in their containers, ethereal and strange. She'd need to run tests, consult with colleagues who specialized in gelatinous zooplankton, see if anyone else along the coast had reported similar blooms.

But that could wait a few hours. She'd been up since five, and her brain was starting to feel like it was swimming through fog of its own.

She rolled her neck, stiff from the morning's work, then sat down at her desk and stared at her phone.

It had been long enough that calling might seem desperate. But long enough, too, that not calling might seem like disinterest.

Before she could overthink it any further, she found Josh's number and hit dial.

He answered on the third ring. "Brenna. Hey."

Just his voice was enough to make her feel slightly ridiculous for all the mental debate that had preceded this moment. He sounded genuinely happy to hear from her, and that alone was enough to make her sit up a little straighter in her chair.

"Hey. I hope I'm not catching you in the middle of something."

"Just finished with a very dramatic Pomeranian who did not appreciate his nail trim. I'm hiding in my office, pretending to do paperwork." A door closed on his end. "His name is Sir Barksalot. I'm not kidding. The owner named him that, and now I have to say it with a straight face. How are you?"

Brenna laughed. "Sir Barksalot. I can't believe you have to say that with a straight face." She shifted the phone to her other ear. "I'm covered in jellyfish slime and questioning my life choices." His laugh made some of the tension in her shoulders ease. "Moon jellyfish bloom down at Twenty-Third Street. Thousands of them washing up on the beach. Plus some lion's mane, which is more concerning."

"I heard something about that on the radio. They were speculating about pollution, toxic runoff—the usual panic."

"It's probably nothing that dramatic, but I won't know until I run some tests. Could be a natural phenomenon, could be environmental. That's the frustrating part of this work—you see something unusual and it can take days, sometimes weeks, to figure out if it matters or not."

"But you'll figure it out. That's what you do."

The confidence in his voice surprised her. They barely knew each other, really. A few encounters at the animal hospital, a handful of text messages, that one conversation about coffee that had never materialized. Yet he spoke as if he already believed in her abilities.

"I try," she said. "Sometimes successfully."

"More than sometimes, I'd guess." He hesitated. "Listen, I'm really glad you called. I was starting to think you'd changed your mind."

"About what?"

"Coffee. Talking about things that aren't turtles. General social interaction outside of emergency wildlife situations."

Brenna leaned back in her chair, letting herself smile. "I haven't changed my mind. I've just been—"

"Busy. I know. Me too. Kitten season is brutal, and I had two emergency surgeries last week. Ate most of my meals standing over the sink because sitting down felt too complicated." He exhaled. "But I keep thinking about it. About you. About that morning when you came to pick up the terrapin. How you talked about your work. I don't know, there was something about it."

Something about it. Brenna knew exactly what he meant, because she'd felt it too—that unexpected sense of connection, the way the conversation had flowed so naturally that she hadn't wanted it to end.

"I keep thinking about it too."

"So let's stop thinking and actually do something. When are you free?"

She pulled up her calendar on her laptop, scanning the next few days. Field work tomorrow morning, a meeting with the Parks Department in the afternoon, volunteer coordination later in the week, a conference call about grant funding.

"This weekend?" she said. "I have Saturday morning blocked for data entry, but I could move that. Or there's the following week."

"Saturday works for me. I'm on call Sunday, but Saturday evening I'm free." She could almost hear him smiling. "I know a place in Margate. If you're interested."

"I'm interested," she said.

"Perfect. Want to meet there around seven?"

"Seven works."

"It's a date, then." When he spoke again, his tone was slightly softer. "An actual date. Not a turtle emergency. Just dinner."

"Just dinner," she agreed. "I'll try not to talk about jellyfish the whole time."

"Talk about whatever you want. I'm just happy you called."

After they hung up, Brenna sat at her desk for a moment, the phone still in her hand. Through the window, she could see the bay stretching toward the horizon, the water ruffled by a light breeze, a sailboat heading for the inlet. A great blue heron stood motionless on the dock, patient as a statue, waiting for something to swim within striking distance.

She had jellyfish samples to process, reports to file, a dozen professional obligations demanding her attention. But underneath all of that, she recognized something she hadn't allowed herself in a while—anticipation. She'd thrown herself into work after her last relationship ended, burying herself in fieldwork and data and early mornings alone. Easier to care about species and ecosystems than to risk caring about another person who might leave.

But Josh didn't feel like a risk, somehow. Or maybe he did, but it was a risk she wanted to take.

The heron on the dock suddenly stabbed its beak into the water and came up with a small fish. It tilted its head back and swallowed, then resumed its patient stance as if nothing had happened.

Brenna smiled. There was a metaphor there somewhere, about patience and timing and knowing when to act. She chose not to examine it too closely.

She turned back to her desk, pulling the samples toward her. Work waited—tests to run, data to collect, a mystery to solve. For once, though, she was looking forward to what lay ahead.

* * *

Maddie wiped a streak of cadmium orange from her forearm with a rag that had seen better days. The canvas before her was coming together—a study of the way fog rolled off the bay on June mornings, making the water and sky seem to blur into a single silver plane. She'd been working on it since eight, chasing the particular glow she'd witnessed last week while walking along the boardwalk.

The gallery wouldn't open for another hour, but Maddie liked these quiet stretches before the crowds descended. It was only her and the paintings and the smell of linseed oil, the soft slap of flip-flops passing on the sidewalk outside.

She stepped back to examine her work, squinting at the place where the horizon should be but wasn't, where everything dissolved into mist. Getting that effect right was proving tricky. Too much definition and the mystery disappeared. Too little and it looked unfinished.

"You're overthinking it," she murmured to herself, setting down her brush. "Let it breathe."

She'd learned that lesson the hard way. Some paintings needed to be wrestled into submission, but others needed space. This one was the latter. She covered her palette, cleaned her brushes, and headed to the small kitchenette in the back to brew a fresh pot.

The kitchenette was barely larger than a closet, big enough for a coffee maker, a mini fridge, a hot plate she rarely used, and a shelf stacked with mismatched mugs collected from thrift stores. Her favorite was a chipped blue one with a faded image of a sandcastle, bought for fifty cents at a garage sale in Margate. It held the right amount of coffee and fit her hand just so.

While she waited, she flipped through the stack of mail that had accumulated over the past few days. Bills, a notice about street cleaning, a postcard from a former gallery visitor who'd moved to Maine and wanted to let her know her painting of the Ocean City sunset was hanging in their living room. Those cards always made her smile. Art found its way into people's lives and became part of their stories, their memories. That was the real reward, more than any sale.

Outside the gallery's front windows, pedestrians walked past. Families with beach chairs and coolers, couples in matching sunhats, kids eating ice cream cones that dripped faster than they could lick. June in Ocean City. The pulse of summer was as familiar to her as her own heartbeat.

By ten o'clock, Coastal Wonders Gallery had welcomed its first visitors of the day—a young couple on their honeymoon who spent twenty minutes admiring the seascapes before buying a small painting of a sandpiper. Maddie wrapped it carefully, chatted with them about the best restaurants in town, and sent them off with recommendations for Brown's for donuts.

The morning settled into its comfortable rhythm. A family

with teenagers wandered through, the kids more interested in their phones than the art until the youngest spotted a painting of the Gillian's Wonderland Ferris wheel and tugged on her mother's sleeve. An older gentleman asked detailed questions about Maddie's technique, a painter himself judging by his inquiries, and they spent a pleasant fifteen minutes discussing the merits of various brush types.

It was nearly noon when a white Mercedes SUV pulled up out front, gleaming like it was fresh from the dealership. The bell over the door chimed, and a woman walked in who immediately stood out from the usual beach crowd.

She was perhaps fifty-six or fifty-seven, with bleach-blond hair swept back from her face in an elegant twist. Her features had a polished, well-maintained quality—full lips, smooth forehead, an ageless look that came from excellent care and likely a skilled dermatologist. Her linen dress was the color of sea foam, simple in cut but clearly expensive, and she wore a single strand of pearls that caught the light as she moved. A Cartier watch glinted on her wrist, and the handbag she carried— Hermès, if Maddie wasn't mistaken—probably cost more than a month's rent. Everything about her suggested old money and easy assurance—someone who didn't need to announce their wealth because it was evident in every gesture.

"Hello," Maddie said, coming out from behind the counter. "Welcome to Coastal Wonders. Please let me know if you have any questions."

The woman gave a slight nod, but her attention was already captured by the large seascape that dominated the gallery's main wall—a painting of the jetty at sunrise that Maddie had finished in April and still considered one of her best pieces.

"This is extraordinary," the woman said, stepping closer. Her voice had the rounded vowels of Philadelphia's Main Line, polished by generations of private schools and country clubs. "The way you've captured the light reflecting off those rocks.

It's not just showing what's there—it's showing what it feels like to be there."

Maddie straightened a little. "Thank you. That jetty gave me trouble. I must have painted it fifty times before I got it right. It's all about catching the exact moment when the sun clears the horizon. Five minutes later and the whole quality of light changes."

"You painted this?" The woman turned to look at Maddie with new interest. "You're the artist?"

"For better or worse." Maddie smiled. "I'm Maddie Scott."

"Lynn Russell." She extended her hand, her grip firm and dry. "I'm down for most of the summer. We have a house in the Riviera. Well, houses in a few places—Palm Beach in the winter, a place in the Berkshires—but Ocean City has always been my favorite. The Hamptons got so crowded." She glanced back at the painting. "How much are you asking for this one?"

Maddie told her the price—it was one of her larger pieces and priced accordingly. Lynn didn't flinch.

"I'll take it." She said it the way someone else might say they'd take a coffee to go. "And I'd like to look at some of your other work. I'm finally redecorating the summer house. We've had the same pieces on the walls for fifteen years, and I'm tired of looking at them. Generic beach scenes that could have been anywhere. Our decorator at the time had no vision—I should have trusted my own eye from the start. I want art that captures Ocean City specifically."

They spent the next forty-five minutes walking through the gallery, Lynn asking thoughtful questions about each painting that interested her. She had a good eye, Maddie realized. She gravitated toward the pieces that had the most emotional resonance rather than the ones that were merely pretty.

By the time they'd made a full circuit, Lynn had selected four additional paintings—a study of beach umbrellas at dusk, a moody interpretation of the Ninth Street Bridge, an intimate close-up of sea grass bending in the wind, and a painting of the boardwalk in winter that Maddie had almost kept for herself.

"These will be perfect," Lynn said, surveying her selections. "They have personality. You can tell these were painted by someone who truly sees Ocean City, not a visitor just passing through."

"I should hope so. I've been coming here since I was a kid, and I've lived here full-time for the past few years."

"It shows in the work." Lynn wandered toward the window, looking out at Asbury Avenue. "I've been to galleries up and down the coast, and I've seen countless paintings of beaches, boats, sunsets. Most of them are perfectly competent and utterly forgettable. Yours stay with you." She faced Maddie again. "Where did you study?"

"I majored in art history at Penn, but the painting is mostly self-taught. I took workshops here and there over the years, learned a lot from other artists, made plenty of mistakes." Maddie shrugged. "Sometimes I think not having formal training was an advantage. I didn't learn the rules, so I couldn't be intimidated by breaking them."

Lynn laughed, a genuine sound of delight. "I like that. My husband is a surgeon. Everything has to be precise, controlled, by the book. It makes him exceptional at his work, but he doesn't always understand the creative impulse." Her expression turned slightly wistful. "He'd be here if he could, but there's always another surgery, another patient who needs him. I've learned to make my own adventures."

"How long have you been married?"

"Thirty years this fall. And I adore him, truly. But somewhere along the way, his career became his life, and I had to decide whether to sit at home waiting for him or build a life of my own." Lynn lifted her chin. "So here I am, at the shore, buying art, keeping busy. He'll come down on weekends when he can." The smile came and went. "But that's quite enough of that. Tell me, do you take commissions?"

"Sometimes. It depends on the project."

"One of my friends has been talking about commissioning something. I think you'd be perfect."

"I'd be happy to discuss it," Maddie said, surprised by how naturally the conversation was flowing. Lynn was easy to talk to, despite her wealth and sophistication. Or perhaps because of it—she asked real questions and actually listened to the answers.

Lynn pulled a sleek card case from her bag and handed one to Maddie. "Now, about delivery. The house is on Glenwood Drive—the address is on the card. Can you arrange to have them brought over?"

Maddie nodded, taking the card. "I can have them delivered tomorrow afternoon, if that works for you."

"Lovely." Lynn paused, studying Maddie with an appraising look. "Tell me something. Do you show your work anywhere else? Other galleries, exhibitions?"

"Things have been moving quickly, actually. A New York museum commissioned a piece from me last fall, and I've had some gallery interest from Philadelphia and Chicago. But this place is still home base. I like being connected to the community here."

Lynn nodded approvingly. "Good for you. It sounds like your career is taking off." She slid a black American Express card across the counter without looking at the total. "I'm having a gathering on my yacht in a few days. Very casual, a small group. I'd love for you to join us."

Maddie blinked. "On your yacht?"

"*The Good Life*. Sixty-two feet, three staterooms, though it's really only me rattling around on it most of the time. She's docked at the Seaview Marina. We'll have cocktails and hors d'oeuvres, watch the sunset over the bay. A handful of my girlfriends—we get together during the summer. Tennis in the mornings, lunch at the club, cocktails on someone's boat. I think you'd be a refreshing addition." Lynn's eyes sparkled.

"Most of them are married to men who work too much, so we've learned to entertain ourselves."

Maddie hesitated. She usually avoided these kinds of things, but curiosity won out. "That's very kind of you. I don't usually—"

"Say yes." Lynn's tone was friendly but firm. "You might surprise yourself."

There was an undeniable appeal to Lynn Russell's combination of elegance and directness. She obviously wasn't someone who was accustomed to hearing no, but nothing about the invitation felt pushy. Just certainty.

"All right," Maddie heard herself say. "I'd like that. Thank you."

"Wonderful." Lynn beamed. "Let's say seven o'clock. Casual but presentable." She signed the credit card receipt with a flourish. "I'll text you the details."

After Lynn left, Maddie stood at the register, slightly dazed. She'd sold more than five thousand dollars' worth of art to a woman she'd met an hour ago, and now she apparently had an invitation to cocktails on a yacht.

CHAPTER FOUR

Lauren had spent every spare moment of the past two days diving deeper into sea glass.

What had started as casual reading after a customer's tip at Romano's had now turned into something closer to obsession. She'd moved past the basic collector forums into auction results and academic articles about historic glass production. She'd learned about pontil marks and embossing patterns, about the difference between genuine sea glass and the tumbled imitations sold in craft stores. And she'd learned about value.

The numbers still didn't feel real.

Cobalt-blue pieces like the ones carpeting their hidden cove regularly sold for fifty to a hundred dollars each. The larger specimens, the ones with interesting shapes or unusual thickness, could fetch even more. Red sea glass, one of the rarest colors, commanded prices in the hundreds. A single piece of true red, properly frosted and of decent size, could sell for three hundred dollars or more to the right collector.

And there were thousands of pieces in that cove. Tens of thousands.

Lauren had done the math on a napkin at Chipper's during a slow moment between breakfast rushes, scribbling figures that made her hand shake. Even a conservative estimate put the value of what they'd found somewhere in the hundreds of thousands of dollars. If she factored in the rarest colors, the number climbed higher still.

She'd shown the napkin to Matt that evening. He'd stared at it for a long moment, then folded it carefully and slipped it into his pocket.

"We need to go back," he'd said.

Now they were finally here, paddling through the early-morning stillness, the sky already a deep blue above them. The bay was calm, barely a ripple disturbing the surface, and they'd timed it for low tide. The exposed rocks of the jetty stretched far out into the water, dark and barnacled in the morning light.

"Narrow passage first, then left," Matt said from behind her.

Lauren nodded, though he couldn't see her. Her arms were tired from the paddle out, but her mind was sharp, alert in a way it hadn't been before. That first visit had been exploration, wonder, discovery. This felt different. This felt like returning to something that was already theirs, even though she knew that wasn't quite true.

The channel opened up before them, and they slipped between the rocks into the maze. Lauren ducked under the same low overhang, felt the same brush of seaweed against her hair. The passage twisted left then right, the rocks pressing close.

They reached the spot where the channel had grown too shallow to paddle on their previous visit. Lauren climbed out into ankle-deep water and pulled her kayak behind her, Matt doing the same. They made their way through the final stretch of the passage, the hulls scraping lightly over sand, until they rounded the last turn and the cove spread out ahead of them.

They pulled the kayaks up onto the beach, well above the waterline, and Lauren took in the scene.

It was just as she remembered. The carpet of sea glass

stretching across the beach, the waves depositing fresh pieces with every surge and retreat, the rock formations curving protectively around the sheltered shore.

"Still here," Matt said, a grin spreading across his face. "I half thought we'd imagined it."

Lauren was already moving toward the glass, kneeling at the water's edge. She ran her fingers through the pieces, the colors even more vivid in the early sun than they'd been three days ago. Deep cobalt. Seafoam green. Amber and brown and white. And there—a flash of red, half-buried beneath a layer of green.

She picked it up. A true red, the size of a quarter, perfectly frosted.

"Matt, look at this."

He dropped down beside her, and she held out the piece. His eyebrows went up. "That's a couple hundred bucks right there."

They got to work. Lauren pulled two plastic bags from her pocket—she'd come prepared this time—and handed one to Matt. She started filling hers with the best pieces. Cobalt after cobalt, more than she'd ever seen in one place. A piece of orange that made her heart skip.

Matt worked beside her, adding to his own bag. Thick chunks of seafoam. Deep amber pieces the color of honey. A purple so dark it was almost black.

"This is unreal," he said, holding up a cobalt piece as big as his palm. "I've never seen one this big."

Lauren hardly looked up. She'd found a pocket of rare colors near the waterline, a concentration of reds and oranges mixed in with the common greens and browns. Her fingers worked quickly, sorting through the glass, pulling out anything worth keeping.

"We should have brought a bucket," she said. "Or a backpack."

"Next time we bring the Jeep."

Lauren laughed—the image of his Jeep navigating the rock maze was absurd. Both bags were already half full. They'd been at it for maybe fifteen minutes and had already collected more valuable sea glass than most people found in a lifetime.

She stood to stretch her back, surveying the beach. They hadn't made a dent. The glass stretched in every direction, layer upon layer of tumbled color, more than two people could collect in a month of mornings.

A breeze kicked up from the south, rustling the grass behind them. And with it came a smell.

Wood smoke. Faint but unmistakable.

"Matt." She kept her voice low. "Do you smell that?"

He straightened, still holding a handful of glass. His expression shifted as he caught the scent. "Yeah. I do."

They both turned toward the dunes.

And that was when Lauren noticed the driftwood.

The bleached driftwood from their first visit—it had been at the top of the shore. Now it sat twenty feet away, near the grass line.

"Someone's been here," she murmured.

Matt's eyes found it too. "The driftwood."

"It moved."

They stood there in silence, scanning the cove for any sign of movement. The beach appeared empty. The dunes rose gently behind them, covered in beach grass and bayberry shrubs. Nothing stirred except the waves.

"The sand," Matt said, gesturing.

Lauren looked. Above the tide line, where the beach transitioned from glass to sand, she could see faint impressions. Footprints. They led from the shoreline up toward the dunes, disappearing into the grass.

"Someone's been walking around," she said. "A lot."

"We should check it out," Matt said.

Lauren hesitated. Part of her wanted to keep collecting—

they'd found so much already, and there was plenty more. But Matt was already setting his bag down and heading inland.

She set her bag beside his and followed.

They crossed the beach toward the dunes where the footprints disappeared. The smoke smell intensified with each step. When they reached the edge of the grass, Matt held up a hand.

"There," he said quietly.

Lauren followed his gaze, and her breath caught in her throat.

Tucked into a hollow between two dunes, partially concealed by beach grass and bayberry bushes, sat a tent. A standard two-person dome tent, the kind you'd find at any outdoor store, its green-and-gray fabric weathered from sun exposure. It wasn't trying to hide, exactly, but the natural dip in the landscape kept it out of sight from the beach.

"Hello?" Matt called out. His voice sounded strange in the quiet cove, too loud after their whispered conversation. "Anyone here?"

No response. The tent flap hung closed, motionless in the still air.

They waited. Thirty seconds. A minute. Nothing.

"They're not here," Matt said.

"But they were." Lauren pointed to a spot just beyond the tent. A ring of stones surrounded a small fire pit, and even from where she stood, she could see the coals inside were still smoldering. Thin wisps of smoke curled up from the ashes.

Lauren stepped closer. A tin mug sat on a rock beside the pit. She bent and touched the side. Still warm.

"Someone was just here," Lauren said. "Within the last hour, maybe less."

Matt went ahead, and Lauren stayed close behind him. As they approached, more details came into view.

A drying line stretched between two scrubby pines, secured with what looked like fishing line. On it hung a worn beach towel, a pair of socks, and a long-sleeved rash guard. All of it washed out and salt-stained, but recently laundered, still damp in the morning air.

Lauren approached the tent, taking in the camp around her. The distant rhythm of waves and the rustle of wind through the beach grass were the only sounds. Whoever was staying here had built an efficient operation in this secluded stretch of shore. A blue tarp had been strung between the tent and a nearby bayberry bush, creating a shaded area where a camp chair sat beside a small folding table. On the table: a battered paperback novel lying face-down, its cover too faded to read, and a water filtration bottle, the kind designed for backcountry hiking.

A pair of binoculars hung from the camp chair's armrest. Lauren followed their sight line—straight down to the beach where she and Matt had been collecting glass minutes earlier.

"Check this out," Matt called.

She turned to find him crouched near a tuft of grass, examining something on the ground. When she joined him, she saw a solar panel the size of a hardcover book, angled toward the sky. A cord ran from it to a phone charger tucked beneath a rock.

"They're here for the long haul," Matt said.

Lauren felt her unease growing. Whoever was staying here had a purpose, had established a base camp while they pursued whatever had brought them here. An adventurer, maybe. Or something else entirely.

Near the fire pit, a small cookstove and a single pot sat on the sand, both showing signs of heavy use. A mesh bag hung from a branch, filled with protein bars and dried fruit. Everything was organized, intentional. Nothing wasted.

A wetsuit was draped over a boulder to dry, along with a nylon duffel. Expensive gear, well-maintained.

But it was what lay beyond the wetsuit that stopped Lauren in her tracks.

Mason jars. A dozen of them, maybe more, arranged in a

neat row on a flat stone. Each one was filled with sea glass, sorted by color with a precision that bordered on obsessive. One held nothing but cobalt-blue pieces, their deep color visible even through the jar. Another contained red and orange, the rarest colors. A third was dedicated to pieces with embossed lettering, fragments of old bottles with partial words still visible.

"Matt," she said, her voice barely above a whisper.

He joined her, exhaling sharply when he saw the jars. "They know exactly what they've found."

Lauren studied the collection without touching it. The sorting was meticulous, professional. The person who'd done this understood sea glass the way Lauren was just beginning to understand it. The cobalt jar alone held enough pieces to fetch several thousand dollars on the collector market. The reds and oranges were worth even more.

"That's a lot of glass," she said, half to herself.

A stack of papers sat beside the mason jars, weighed down by a smooth gray stone. Lauren lifted the stone carefully and examined the top sheet.

Tide charts. Printed from some website, with specific times circled in pen. High tides and low tides for the current week, all marked and annotated in handwriting she didn't recognize. Notes in the margins: "channel passable" next to one low tide, "too rough" next to another.

"They're timing their trips through the channel," Lauren said. "They know the cove better than we do."

She flipped to the next page. More tide charts, these ones for the previous week. The pattern was clear: the camper had been tracking the tides carefully, learning the rhythm of this place, understanding exactly when it was safe to come and go.

Lauren set the papers back in place and stood up, looking around the camp with new eyes. This person had dedicated themselves to the cove and its treasure with single-minded focus.

A sound made Lauren freeze.

It came from somewhere behind her, beyond the dunes. A rustling. Footsteps on sand.

She grabbed Matt's arm, and they both went still, listening. The sound came again, closer this time. The crunch of grass being pressed down by weight. Movement through the brush.

Lauren's heart pounded so hard she could feel it in her throat. Her eyes met Matt's, and she saw her own fear reflected there. They were exposed here, standing in the middle of someone else's camp, surrounded by their belongings.

The sound stopped.

They waited. Ten seconds. Twenty. The silence stretched out. No footsteps. No voice.

Nothing moved.

"Wind," Matt said finally, though he didn't sound convinced. "Just the wind."

Lauren agreed, but she couldn't shake the feeling that they were being watched. That somewhere in those dunes, eyes were on them.

"We should go," she said.

Matt didn't argue. They backed away from the camp slowly, retracing their steps across the sand, through the tall grass, back toward the beach. Lauren kept glancing over her shoulder, certain she would see a figure emerging from the dunes, but the camp remained still and empty behind them.

When they reached the spot where they'd left their bags, Lauren grabbed hers. Matt scooped up his own. The heft of it was satisfying in her hand. Whatever else had happened this morning, they weren't leaving empty-handed.

They continued to the kayaks and pushed off into the shallows. The passage out felt quicker than the way in, their strokes more sure now that they knew the route. They emerged into open water as the sun climbed higher over Ocean City.

"So someone else found it," Matt said, pulling his kayak alongside hers. "Set up camp."

"And they mean business. That's not a casual beach-comber. That's someone with a plan."

They paddled in silence for a while, the familiar shoreline sliding past. A tern dove into the water nearby, coming up empty and circling for another try.

Lauren patted the plastic bag tucked between her feet. "We did pretty well ourselves."

"Not bad for a quick stop."

Matt was quiet for a moment, his paddle dipping steadily. "I was thinking—before, I figured we'd eventually tell people about this."

Lauren nodded. She'd had similar thoughts. The cove was too big for two people to harvest alone, and sharing it had seemed like the obvious next step.

"But now..." Matt trailed off.

"Now there's someone living there."

"Yeah." He glanced back toward the jetty, though the cove was long out of sight. "I don't want to bring a crowd into that. Feels wrong."

Lauren understood. Whatever the camper's story was, they'd carved out something private in that tucked-away stretch of shore. Showing up with a group would shatter that—turn the cove into a free-for-all.

"There's more glass than we could collect in a summer," she said. "And the tide keeps bringing in more. We can wait until we figure out what's going on."

"Agreed." Matt pulled his paddle across his lap, letting the kayak drift for a moment. "Just us for now."

"How do you think they found it?" Lauren asked. "The camper, I mean. Same way we did?"

Matt considered this. "Maybe. Or maybe they knew to look for it. Those tide charts weren't just for getting through the channel—they had notes about conditions. Like they'd been studying the area."

"You think they knew the cove was there before they found it?"

"I don't know. But someone that organized doesn't just stumble onto things."

They paddled on, the rhythm of their strokes falling into sync. Lauren found herself thinking about the smoldering coals, the clothes still damp on the line. The camper had been close by when they'd arrived. Maybe watching.

"Do you think they saw us?" she asked.

Matt didn't answer right away. "Probably. That sound we heard in the dunes—I don't think it was the wind."

Lauren had wondered the same thing. "They might not want us there."

"Maybe not." Matt shrugged, his paddle catching the light. "But they don't own the place. It's public land, same as any beach."

"Still. We were going through their stuff."

"We were looking. There's a difference." He paused. "If we run into them next time, we just talk to them. See what they're about."

Lauren wasn't sure it would be that simple. Someone who'd gone to that much trouble to stake out a place like that might not welcome company. But there was no point worrying about it now.

They rounded the curve of the shoreline, the Tennessee Avenue boat ramp coming into view in the distance. A handful of boats dotted the water now, fishermen trying their luck in the bay.

"We should go back," Matt said. "See if we can figure out more about them."

Lauren nodded. The cove wasn't theirs alone anymore—maybe it never had been. She was curious about the camper, sure. But mostly she was thinking about all that glass, glittering on the sand, waiting to be collected.

CHAPTER FIVE

Nancy had been looking forward to this interview all week.

Tony Russo had cut hair in Ocean City for over fifty years. His shop on Asbury Avenue had been a fixture since 1965, and according to everyone Nancy had spoken to, Tony had heard more secrets in that barber chair than a priest in a confessional. He'd finally retired a few years back, but the stories—so local legend went—were still sharp as his scissors.

Joe had made the connection. Tony had been cutting his father's hair since the 1970s, and even now he showed up at Chipper's most mornings for coffee and eggs, sitting at the same counter stool he'd claimed decades ago. When Joe mentioned the podcast, Tony had waved him off at first—"I'm no storyteller"—but Joe had persisted, and eventually Tony agreed to one interview. Just one.

"He won't talk about the real stuff," Joe had warned her that morning. "Old-school guys like Tony, they take discretion seriously. You'll get the sanitized version."

Nancy had suspected the same thing. Joe sat in on all her interviews, for technical and moral support. Today she was especially glad to have him there. Joe had a way with men of a certain generation. They trusted him. Something about the way he listened without judgment, the way he could turn a conversation toward deeper waters without anyone noticing.

Now Tony sat across from her at the dining room table, the microphone positioned between them. He was eighty-four but looked a decade younger, with a full head of jet-black hair that he clearly dyed himself—an advertisement for his profession, Nancy supposed—and hands that still looked steady enough to handle a straight razor. He wore a bright-purple button-down shirt open at the collar, revealing a thatch of gray chest hair and three gold chains of varying thickness. His pinky ring caught the light when he gestured.

"Before we start," Tony said, eyeing the microphone, "I want to be clear. I'm not here to gossip. Some things people told me in that chair, they stay with me. You understand?"

"Absolutely," Nancy said, keeping her voice steady. There was something about Tony that made her want to choose her words carefully—the way he held himself, the directness of his gaze. He reminded her of characters from those old mob movies, the kind of men who knew people and never had to raise their voices because they didn't need to. "We're interested in your memories of Ocean City. The characters, the changes you've seen. Nothing you're not comfortable sharing."

Tony nodded, seemingly satisfied. "All right then. What do you want to know?"

Nancy pressed record. "Let's start at the beginning. How did you end up in Ocean City?"

Tony settled back in his chair. "My father was a barber in South Philly. Learned the trade from him, started cutting hair when I was sixteen. But the city was getting crowded, you know? Too many shops, not enough customers. Then my uncle, he had this little building on Asbury Avenue that wasn't being used. Said I could have it cheap if I fixed it up myself."

"So you took a chance."

"Biggest gamble of my life." Tony smiled. "I was twenty-three years old, didn't know a soul down here. But I figured, beach town, tourists in summer, locals year-round—there'd always be hair to cut."

"And there was."

"Over fifty years' worth." He shook his head slowly. "I cut hair for three generations of some families. Grandfather, father, son. Watched boys turn into men in that chair. Some of them, I cut their hair for their wedding day, then years later for their kid's christening."

Joe leaned forward from his spot at the end of the table. "That's a lot of conversations over the years."

"More than I can count. You know how it is in a barber shop. People talk. Sitting in that chair, the cape around their neck, the sound of the scissors—it relaxes them. They say things they might not say anywhere else."

"Like what?" Joe asked, his tone casual.

Tony glanced at him, then back at Nancy. "Stories. Memories. Sometimes complaints about their wives." He chuckled. "Harmless stuff, mostly."

Nancy nodded. This was the sanitized version Joe had predicted. Charming, but surface-level. She decided to try a different approach.

"I've heard from a few people around town," Nancy said, "that you know more about what really went on in Ocean City than anyone else."

Something flickered in Tony's eyes. "People talk too much." He studied his hands. "But I've been around a long time. You hear things, sitting in that chair all day. People forget you're even there after a while."

"What were the old days like?"

"Different. Smaller. Everyone knew everyone's business, but we pretended we didn't." Tony looked toward the window, his gaze distant. "There was a code back then. What happened in Ocean City stayed in Ocean City. Especially the stuff that wasn't supposed to happen at all."

Joe shifted in his chair. "What kind of stuff?"

Tony turned to look at him, and Nancy saw something pass between them—an unspoken understanding. Two men of a certain age, speaking a language that didn't require words.

"Let me tell you about Vinnie Cannoli," Tony said finally. He caught Nancy's look and waved a hand. "That's not his real name, obviously. But you want the story, I'll give you the story. Just not the name." He adjusted one of his gold chains. "This was, oh, 1985 or thereabouts. Vinnie was a regular customer. Nice enough guy, maybe forty years old. Ran a little insurance office on Ocean Avenue. Wife, two kids, house in the Gardens."

Joe nodded slowly, something shifting in his expression. "I think I know who you're talking about. His wife was friends with my mother."

"That's right. His wife was a good woman. Patient. Had to be, married to Vinnie." He leaned back. "Vinnie liked the ponies. Loved them, actually. Couldn't stay away from the track. And when he couldn't get to the track, he found other ways to place his bets."

The interview had moved into new territory. Nancy stayed quiet, letting Tony find his own way into the story.

"One summer, Vinnie got himself into trouble. Real trouble. Owed money to people you don't want to owe money to. He came into the shop looking like he hadn't slept in a week. Told me he didn't know what he was going to do. Said if something didn't change, they were going to break his legs—or worse."

"What happened?" Joe asked.

Tony was quiet for a long moment. "Week later, Vinnie went swimming off Thirty-Fourth Street. Got caught in a riptide. They found his clothes on the beach, his wallet, his watch. Never found the body."

Nancy leaned forward. "He drowned?"

"That's what everyone said. That's what the papers printed. The wife collected the life insurance, moved the kids to her sister's place in Haddonfield. Tragic accident, everyone said. Poor Vinnie."

Tony reached for the glass of water Nancy had set out and took a long drink.

"Five years later," he continued, "I'm at my nephew's wedding in Nashville. Tennessee, if you can believe it. Nice hotel downtown. And I see a man at the bar who looks familiar. Older, heavier, different haircut. But I've been cutting hair my whole life—I know faces. And I know Vinnie Cannoli's face."

Nancy felt a chill run through her despite the June heat outside. "You're saying he faked his death?"

"I'm saying I saw him drinking a martini at a hotel bar in Nashville five years after he supposedly drowned." Tony set down his glass. "He saw me too. We looked at each other for maybe two seconds. Then he picked up his drink and walked out. Never looked back."

"Did you report it?" Nancy asked.

"Report what? I saw a man who looked like someone I used to know. That's not a crime." Tony's eyes hardened. "And even if I was sure, I don't report things. You start talking to cops, to authorities, you bring trouble on yourself. That's not how I was raised." He shrugged. "Besides, the wife had moved on by then. Remarried, happy. Those kids had processed their grief and started new lives. What good would it do to dredge all that up?"

Joe tilted his head. "Sometimes the truth does more harm than good."

"That's what I figured. Wasn't my business anyway."

"Were there other stories like that?" she asked carefully. "Things you saw that you never told anyone?"

Tony laughed, but there was no humor in it. "Honey, I could fill a book. But most of it—" He shook his head. "Most of it needs to stay buried."

"What about things that don't need to stay buried?" Joe

asked. "Stories about people who are gone now. Things that can't hurt anyone anymore."

Tony considered this. His gaze drifted.

"There was a photography studio on the boardwalk," he said after a moment. "Peterson's Portraits. You remember it, Joe?"

Joe squinted, searching his memory. "Vaguely. They did the family photos, right? The ones with the fake beach backgrounds?"

"That's the place. Lou Peterson ran it from the mid-fifties until he disappeared in sixty-eight. Vanished overnight. One day the shop was open, the next it was empty. Everyone assumed he'd gotten into financial trouble and skipped town."

"But that wasn't it," Nancy said.

"No." Tony's voice dropped lower. "Lou had a side business. He had a long-range lens, used to set up in the dunes near certain motels. The kind of motels where people went when they didn't want to be seen together."

Nancy's stomach tightened. "He was photographing affairs."

"Photographing them and selling the pictures back to the people in them. Twenty dollars, fifty dollars, sometimes more depending on how much they had to lose. Operated for years before anyone caught on."

"How did you find out?"

"One of my customers was on the receiving end. Came into the shop white as a sheet, told me the whole story. He'd been stepping out on his wife with a woman from Mays Landing. Next thing he knows, there's an envelope in his mailbox with photos and a note about how much it would cost to make sure his wife never saw them."

"That's blackmail," Joe said.

"That's exactly what it was. But who was going to report it? You report it, the whole thing comes out. Your marriage, your reputation, everything. Lou understood that. He picked his targets carefully—people with too much to lose."

"So what happened to him?" Nancy asked. "You said he disappeared."

Tony paused. "The story I heard—and this is just what I heard, mind you—is that Lou made the mistake of photographing the wrong person. Someone connected. Someone whose family didn't take kindly to being shaken down."

"Connected how?"

"Use your imagination." Tony's expression was unreadable. "All I know is, one night Lou Peterson closed up his shop like normal, and no one ever saw him again. His car was still parked behind the building the next morning. His apartment was untouched. It was like he'd stepped off the edge of the earth."

The room felt very still. Nancy realized she'd been holding her breath.

"The shop sat empty for two years," Tony continued. "Nobody wanted to buy it—people said it was cursed. Eventually someone from out of state picked it up, turned it into a T-shirt shop. But for a while there, everyone walked a little faster when they passed that building."

Joe was quiet. "I had no idea."

"Nobody did. That was the whole point." Tony turned to Nancy. "You wanted to know what Ocean City was really like back then? It was like anywhere else. Good people doing their best, and some not-so-good people taking advantage. The difference is, in this beach town, the secrets have a way of staying secret. Everyone's got something to hide, so everyone agrees to look the other way."

Nancy thought about what Jean had said in her interview. Ocean City's got layers. Good people who did questionable things. Questionable people who did good things.

"Tell her about the Rossis and the Wilsons," Joe said quietly.

Tony's eyebrows rose. "You know about that?"

"Bits and pieces. My father mentioned it once, but he wouldn't give me details."

"Your father was a smart man." Tony drummed his fingers on the table then pointed at the laptop. "Turn that off."

Nancy hesitated. "The recording?"

"This one's not for your podcast. The Rossis and Wilsons—they're still here. Still got money, still got influence. You air something like this, you're not just telling a story. You're poking a hornet's nest." He crossed his arms. "You want to hear the story, I'll tell you. But it stays in this room."

Nancy glanced at Joe, who gave a slight nod. They already had more than enough material—Vinnie Cannoli alone was a bombshell. And truthfully, she wanted to hear this for herself, not just for the podcast.

She clicked the stop button. The red recording light went dark.

"Off," she said. "Just us."

He studied her briefly, then nodded.

"The Rossis and the Wilsons were two of the oldest families in Ocean City. Both arrived in the early 1900s, both made their money in real estate, both thought they owned the town. For a while, they were friendly—business partners, even. Franklin Rossi and Thomas Wilson built the Parker Hotel together in the twenties. Owned a whole block of rental properties on the south end."

"What happened?"

"What always happens. A woman." Tony's voice was matter-of-fact. "In 1962, Thomas Wilson's wife, Sofia, started an affair with Franklin Rossi's son, Robert. Robert was twenty-eight, handsome, charming. Sofia was forty-one, bored, and married to a man who cared more about money than he did about her."

"How long did it last?"

"About a year and a half, from what I understand. They weren't exactly careful about it—half the town knew before Thomas did. When he finally found out, things got ugly fast."

Joe exhaled. "I can imagine."

"No, you can't." Tony leaned forward. "Thomas Wilson was not a forgiving man. He filed for divorce, which was scandalous enough in those days. But that wasn't enough for him. He wanted to destroy the Rossis completely."

"How?"

"First, he pulled out of every joint business venture. Cost both families a fortune, but Thomas didn't care—he had enough money to survive the loss, and he knew the Rossis were more leveraged. Then he started buying up properties the Rossis wanted, just to keep them from expanding. For two years, it was open warfare."

Nancy's mind was racing, trying to keep up with all the names and dates. "Did it stay at that level? Business warfare?"

Tony's expression darkened. "No. It got worse." He lowered his voice. "Summer of 1965. The Parker—the Rossis had kept it in the split and renamed it the Rossi Hotel—burned to the ground. Middle of the night, no fatalities, thank the Lord. Fire marshal ruled it electrical, but nobody believed that."

"They thought Thomas Wilson was responsible?"

"I'm not saying he lit the match himself. But the timing was awfully convenient. And Thomas had the resources to make things happen without getting his own hands dirty."

"Was there ever any proof?"

"Not that I know of. But Franklin Rossi believed it with his whole heart. He spent the rest of his life trying to prove Thomas was behind it. Died in 1978 still swearing he'd get justice someday."

"And the families?"

"Never spoke again. Still don't, as far as I know. The younger generations, they probably don't even know why they're supposed to hate each other. Just that they do." Tony sighed. "That's how feuds work. The original sin gets forgotten, but the anger gets passed down like an inheritance."

This was not the Ocean City she'd thought she knew.

Tony stood. "I'm eighty-four. Most of these people are gone. Figured someone should know before I'm gone too." He headed for the door without another word.

After Tony left, Nancy and Joe sat in silence for a while.

"Well," Joe said at last. "That was something."

"That was a lot of something." Nancy glanced at the laptop. "And we got most of it on tape."

She was already thinking about how to structure the episode. The Vinnie Cannoli story was gold—a man faking his own death to escape gambling debts, spotted years later at a hotel bar in Nashville. Listeners would eat that up. And Lou Peterson's blackmail operation, ending with his mysterious disappearance? That was the kind of story that got people sharing episodes with their friends.

"This might be our best one yet," she said.

Joe grinned. "Jean's going to be jealous."

Nancy began packing up the equipment. The Rossi-Wilson story would stay between them—Tony had made that clear—but the rest of it was fair game. Tony had come here to talk, and talk he did.

Ocean City had secrets. And now, thanks to Tony Russo, some of them were about to go public.

* * *

Claire should have known better.

After the disaster with Glen, she'd told herself to take time off from the app. But by the end of the evening, she'd convinced herself not to let one bad date ruin her momentum.

She'd reopened the app before bed.

Todd had seemed promising. His profile was understated—

no shirtless gym selfies, no fish he'd caught, no manifestos about what he was looking for in a partner. Just a few nice photos, a mention that he worked in marketing, and a bio that said he was "looking for someone to share adventures with."

Adventures sounded nice. Adventures sounded healthy.

Their messages had been pleasant. Flirty without being aggressive. He'd suggested mini golf for their first date, which Claire appreciated—it was casual, well-lit, and had plenty of people around.

The mini golf course was on the bay side of the island, one of those places with a dinosaur theme and a T-rex that never quite roared right. Claire arrived five minutes early and found Todd already waiting by the entrance, holding two putters and looking genuinely happy to see her.

"Claire! You made it!" He handed her a putter with a flourish. "I already got us set up. I hope you're ready to lose."

"Pretty confident for a first date." Claire smiled, starting to relax. This was fine. This was normal.

"I should warn you—I was the mini golf champion of my summer camp three years running." Todd held the gate open for her. "Ages eight through ten. Very prestigious."

"I'm trembling."

They started on the first hole, a simple straight shot with a T-rex's mouth at the end. Claire sank it in two strokes. Todd took four, his ball bouncing off the dinosaur's teeth twice before finally rolling in.

"Okay," he said, marking his score. "So maybe I've lost a step since camp."

By the third hole, Claire was actually having fun. Todd was funny without trying too hard, self-deprecating about his golf skills, and interested in getting to know her rather than just talking about himself. When she mentioned her kids, he asked thoughtful follow-up questions. When she talked about her separation, he listened without offering unsolicited advice.

This was going well. Really well.

Then they reached the seventh hole.

It was the one with the volcano, the ball meant to spiral up a ramp and drop through a tunnel into the hole below. Claire was lining up her shot when she heard it.

"Claire."

She looked up. Todd was standing in the middle of the course, putter at his side, staring at her with an intensity that hadn't been there a moment ago.

"I need to tell you something."

She straightened, uneasy. "Okay?"

"I know we just met. But I believe in being honest, and I have to say—I think there's something really special here. Between us."

Claire blinked. She waited for the punchline, for that goofy grin to break across his face. It didn't come. "We've known each other for twenty minutes."

"I know! But sometimes you just know, you know?" His eyes were shining. "I've been waiting to meet someone like you for a long time. And I have a good sense about these things."

A family with two young kids was trying to play through, the father shooting Claire apologetic looks as he herded them around Todd's stationary form.

"Maybe we should keep playing?" Claire suggested.

"Yes! Absolutely!" Todd moved to his ball, but he kept talking as he lined up his shot. "I was actually thinking—my company has this retreat in the Poconos next month. Partners are invited. There's a spa."

He swung. His ball sailed past the volcano entirely and landed in a small tar pit.

"Whoops." He shrugged. "Anyway, the retreat. What do you think?"

"Todd, that's next month."

"I know, but I feel like I already know you." He retrieved his ball from the tar pit—really just a shallow pond painted black—seemingly unbothered by the water soaking his shoes.

"We have so much in common. Like, you're a runner—I saw you did a half marathon back in 2019. I've done a few 5Ks myself. And we clearly have the same taste in food. That Thai place in Somers Point? You were totally right about the pad thai."

Claire felt something cold settle in her stomach. "How do you know all that?"

"I did a little research." He said it like it was charming. "Your LinkedIn, some other stuff. I like to know who I'm meeting. It's just being prepared."

"That's..." Claire searched for the right word. A quick Google before a date was one thing. This was something else. "That's really unsettling, actually."

"I'm thorough." Todd grinned, rejoining her on the path with wet footprints trailing behind him. "My therapist says I have a gift for focus. When I find something I want, I go all in."

They made it to the eighth hole, a complicated setup involving a pterodactyl with moving wings. Claire was trying to figure out how to extract herself when Todd reached for his phone.

"Hold on—I want to capture this moment." He angled himself next to her, holding the phone up for a selfie. "For our story. When people ask how we met, we'll show them this picture and say it all started on a dinosaur-themed mini golf course."

"Are you serious right now?"

He snapped the photo anyway.

"Perfect." He was already typing something. "I'm just going to post this real quick. My mom is going to be so excited."

"You're posting that?"

"It's just for my mom. She's my best friend—she'll love it." Todd finished typing and slid his phone back into his pocket. "She can't wait to meet you. I was thinking maybe next weekend? She makes an incredible lasagna."

"Todd." Claire held up a hand. "This isn't working."

"What do you mean?"

"I mean you dug through my entire online history and then told me about it. You're talking about meeting your mother. You just posted a photo of us without asking. This is too much."

Todd's expression shifted. The eager warmth drained away, replaced by something tighter. "Okay. Wow."

"I'm sorry, I just—"

"No, no. I get it." He held up his hands. "I mean, I thought we had a connection, but clearly I misread the situation. It happens." He paused. "I guess I shouldn't be surprised. Your profile did say you were 'figuring things out.' I just thought you were further along in the process."

Claire stared at him. "Excuse me?"

"I'm just saying, some people aren't ready to meet someone who's actually emotionally available. It's fine. You'll get there eventually." He gave her a look that was somehow both pitying and condescending. "Maybe try therapy? It really helps."

"I'm going to go."

"That's probably for the best." Todd picked up his ball and examined it. "I hope you find what you're looking for, Claire. I really do. Even if you don't know what that is yet."

She set her putter against the velociraptor and headed for the exit. Behind her, she heard him call out.

"Good luck out there! Dating's tough for women your age!"

She didn't look back.

In her car, Claire locked the doors and stared at the glow of the mini golf course's neon dinosaur sign. Her phone buzzed. A message from Todd: I'm sorry if I came on too strong. Can we start over? I'll tone it down. Also my mom says hi.

She deleted it.

Her phone buzzed again. Another message: I understand if you need space. Just know that I'll be here when you're ready. Forever, if necessary.

She blocked him.

For a long moment, she just sat there, processing the evening. Glen had been insufferable, but at least his self-absorption had been predictable. Todd was something else entirely—earnest and creepy and condescending all at once, somehow convinced he was the emotionally mature one.

Her phone buzzed a third time. She almost threw it out the window before realizing it was a text from her sister: How was the date?

Claire typed back: I'm retiring from dating. Permanently.

The response came instantly: That bad?

He told me he'd researched my half marathon and found a restaurant review I left. Then suggested I try therapy. Then yelled "good luck, dating's tough for women your age" as I walked away.

A string of laughing emojis appeared, followed by: I need to hear this whole story. Call me.

Claire started the car and pulled out of the parking lot, already composing the story in her head. It would be funny tomorrow, honestly. She'd tell her sister, her friends, and they'd laugh and shake their heads, and she'd laugh too.

But tonight, heading home, she wasn't laughing.

CHAPTER SIX

The call came in just after eight in the morning, and it wasn't good news.

"We've got man o' war," Lieutenant Morrison said, his voice edged with disbelief. "Twenty-Eighth Street, Thirty-Fourth Street—they're washing up all over the island now. It's not just the moon jellies anymore."

Brenna sat up straighter. "Man o' war? Are you sure?"

"Positive. Those bright-blue floats are hard to miss." Morrison paused. "I've seen maybe two man o' war in all my years here, both strays. This is something else."

"How many are we talking about?"

"Enough to close beaches up and down the island. And there's a situation. A tourist ignored the warnings at Thirty-Fourth Street. Got stung pretty bad. Ambulance took him to the hospital about an hour ago."

Brenna's stomach dropped. Portuguese man o' war weren't technically jellyfish at all but siphonophores, colonial organisms made up of specialized polyps working together. The distinction was academic to most people, but the danger was very real. Their tentacles could trail thirty feet or more below the surface, and the venom was powerful enough to cause cardiac arrest in severe cases.

Morrison sighed heavily. "It's already all over social media. Going to be a circus today."

"I'm on my way."

She grabbed her keys and her field kit and was out the door in under a minute. By the time she reached Thirty-Fourth Street, she could see the crowd gathered near the lifeguard stand, phones raised to capture whatever was happening on the sand.

Red flags flew from every stand she could see, the universal signal for dangerous conditions. Lifeguards were stationed at intervals along the beach, waving people back from the water's edge. Brenna parked and made her way through the onlookers, some still in their swimsuits, beach chairs abandoned behind them.

The scene on the sand confirmed her fears. Man o' war dotted the shoreline, their vivid blue floats standing out among the more familiar translucent bodies of moon jellies. The color was almost electric against the pale sand, purple-blue sails that looked like they belonged in the Caribbean, not New Jersey.

"I've never seen anything like this," she said, more to herself than anyone. "They shouldn't be here. Not in these numbers."

"Don't touch them," she called out to a young beach patrol officer who was getting too close. "Even dead, they can still sting. We need full protective gear before we handle anything."

She spent the next three hours documenting the bloom, collecting samples, and coordinating with beach patrol up and down the island. The man o' war had appeared seemingly overnight, carried in by currents that should have kept them far offshore. Something was shifting in the water, drawing creatures inland that belonged in the open ocean.

By noon, the situation was under control but far from resolved. The beaches remained closed, red flags still flying, and Brenna knew they would stay that way until she could confirm the waters were safe. Families who had planned beach days lingered near the dunes, children whining about the unfairness of it all.

She called her supervisor from the truck, giving him a detailed report of everything she'd observed. Word came back that the man who'd been stung was stable but still in the hospital, his arm and chest covered in angry red welts where the tentacles had brushed against him.

"He went in despite the warnings," Morrison had told her. "Said he didn't believe it could be that serious. His wife was screaming at him the whole way into the ambulance."

People always thought they knew better. That the rules didn't apply to them, that nature's dangers were exaggerated for the timid. Sometimes they got lucky. Sometimes they didn't.

Brenna headed back to the research station with her samples secured in the back of the truck, her mind already running through the tests she'd need to conduct. The bloom was spreading, and without understanding why, she had no way to predict what would come next.

Her phone buzzed. A text from Josh: *Still on for tonight? I made reservations.*

She smiled despite everything. In all the chaos of the morning, she'd almost forgotten about their dinner plans. Steve and Cookie's in Margate. A real date, not just coffee or a quick hello at the animal hospital.

Absolutely, she typed back. *Wouldn't miss it.*

His response came immediately: *Looking forward to it.*

The knot in her chest loosened just a little. Whatever else was happening in the waters around Ocean City, she had tonight.

* * *

Steve and Cookie's occupied a corner spot on Amherst Avenue, its windows glowing against the deepening dusk. Brenna had changed three times before settling on a simple navy dress that she hoped struck the right balance between trying too hard and not trying enough.

Josh was already there when she arrived, waiting outside with his hands in his pockets. He looked different out of his scrubs, more relaxed somehow, wearing a button-down shirt with the sleeves rolled to his elbows and khaki pants that actually fit well.

"You made it," he said, his face breaking into a smile that made her feel instantly at ease. "I was worried the jellyfish might win."

"They tried. I'm stubborn."

He held the door for her, and they were led to a table by the window, the kind of spot that would have been reserved weeks in advance during peak season. The restaurant was busy but not packed, conversations humming at neighboring tables, the clink of glassware providing pleasant background music.

"I've been wanting to try this place," Josh admitted once they'd ordered drinks.

"I've heard good things," Brenna said, settling her napkin in her lap. "Haven't had a chance to try it yet."

"Well, here we are." He raised his water glass in a mock toast. "Finally giving ourselves a good reason."

They ordered a couple of appetizers and took their time with the entree menu. When the wine arrived, a pinot noir that the server recommended, Brenna felt the last of the day's tension start to drain away.

"Tell me about the jellyfish," Josh said. "The real version, not the news version."

So she did. She told him about the moon jellies and the man o' war, about the shifting currents and the mystery of why creatures were appearing where they shouldn't be. The tourist who'd ignored the warnings and ended up in the hospital.

Josh listened with genuine interest, asking questions that showed he actually understood the science, or at least wanted to. He didn't offer solutions or try to minimize the problem the way some people did when she talked about her work. He just listened.

"It sounds frustrating," he said when she finished. "Knowing something's wrong but not knowing why."

"That's the job, half the time. Observing patterns, collecting data, waiting for the picture to come into focus." She took a sip of wine. "What about you? How did you end up as a vet in Ocean City?"

"Long story or short story?"

"We've got time."

He smiled at that. "I grew up in Pitman—small town about an hour west of here. Suburban kid, completely landlocked. But my grandmother had a place in Margate, and we'd come down every summer. I fell in love with the shore. The beach, the boardwalk, all of it. I always said I'd find a way to live here someday."

"So you did."

"Eventually." He grinned. "Though I'll admit, vet school didn't exactly prepare me for shore life. You'd be amazed how many dogs think crabs are chew toys. They see something scuttling across the sand, and their brain just shuts off. Every summer I get at least a dozen dogs with pinched noses, pinched paws, one memorable case of a pinched tongue."

Brenna laughed. "The crab won that round."

"The crab absolutely won." He shook his head. "But the best was last August. A woman comes in with her parrot—big African Grey, beautiful bird—for a routine nail trim. My technician opens the carrier, and the bird just rockets out. I mean, gone. Flying laps around the waiting room."

"No."

"There are dogs barking, cats hissing, a rabbit having what I can only describe as a nervous breakdown. My receptionist is ducking behind the desk. And the whole time, this parrot is circling the room, screeching 'Bad dog! Bad dog!' at the top of its lungs."

Brenna was laughing now, really laughing. "How did you catch it?"

"We didn't. It finally landed on a ceiling fan—which, thankfully, was off—and just sat there judging us for twenty minutes until it got bored and flew back to its owner." He leaned back in his chair. "She didn't even apologize. Just said, 'He needed to stretch his wings.'"

"I think I love that woman."

"She's one of my favorite clients. Completely unhinged, but the bird's always healthy."

They were both still smiling when he continued. "Anyway. I went to Delaware for undergrad, then vet school at Cornell. Worked at a practice in Philadelphia for a few years, trying to pay off loans and build experience." He paused, something shifting in his expression. "Then my marriage ended, and I decided it was time to make a change."

Brenna set down her wine glass. "I didn't know you'd been married."

"It was a while ago. We were young. Too young, probably. Met in vet school, got married right after graduation, thought we'd figure out the rest as we went." He shrugged. "Turned out we had different ideas about the future. She wanted a practice in Manhattan, fancy clients, designer dogs. I was looking for something quieter."

"I'm sorry."

"Don't be. It was the right decision for both of us. She's happy now, remarried, living the life she always pictured." He smiled. "And I'm here, which is exactly where I want to be."

The appetizers arrived—littleneck clams and a roasted beet salad to share. They both reached for the clams at the same time and laughed.

"Go ahead," Josh said.

Brenna took one. He was quiet for a moment, turning his wine glass by the stem.

"There's something else, though. I was engaged. More recently. Last year. We'd been together for two years, set a date, the whole thing." He shifted in his seat. "I called it off about eight months ago."

"What happened?"

"I realized I was going through the motions. She was great on paper, but something was missing. It wasn't fair to either of us to keep pretending." He looked at her directly. "I'm not proud of how long it took me to figure that out."

Brenna sat with that for a moment. A broken engagement eight months ago. That was different than a marriage that ended years back. It made her wonder if he was really ready, or if she was just the next person to come along.

"I appreciate you telling me," she said.

Their entrees arrived—salmon for Brenna, the jumbo lump crab cake for Josh. They talked about the food, about the restaurant, easing back into lighter territory.

They finished their meal with easier conversation. When the check came, Josh insisted on paying, and Brenna let him.

Outside, they stood on the sidewalk for a moment.

"I had a really nice time," Josh said.

"So did I." And she meant it.

He leaned in and kissed her cheek, a gesture that was sweet and tentative and exactly right for where they were. Then he walked to his car, and she walked to hers, and they drove in opposite directions through the quiet streets of Margate.

* * *

The marina at Seaview was a different world entirely.

Maddie had driven past this stretch of the bay hundreds of times over the years, had noticed the boats lined up at the docks, but she'd never had reason to stop. Now, walking down the main pier past small fishing boats and sailboats, a box of chocolates in one hand and her purse in the other, she found herself heading toward the far end, where the slips grew wider and the vessels more impressive.

The Good Life was impossible to miss. Sixty-two feet of sleek fiberglass and polished teak, it dominated the end slip like a queen holding court. Lynn Russell stood on the back deck in white linen pants and a silk blouse the color of coral, waving enthusiastically when she spotted Maddie approaching.

"You made it!" Lynn called out. "Come aboard, come aboard."

A uniformed crew member appeared at the gangway, offering his hand to help Maddie step onto the boat. The transition from dock to deck felt oddly ceremonial, like crossing some invisible threshold into a world where the rules were different.

"I brought chocolates," Maddie said, holding up the box as Lynn clasped her hand in greeting.

Lynn glanced at the box and smiled approvingly. "How thoughtful. But darling, you should have brought yourself and nothing else." She linked her arm through Maddie's and steered her toward the stern. "Now, let me introduce you to everyone."

The back deck had been transformed into an elegant outdoor living room. Plush cushions in shades of cream and navy covered the built-in seating, and a low table held an array of hors d'oeuvres that looked like they belonged in a magazine spread. Silver serving dishes sat alongside crystal glasses that caught the early evening light.

Four women were already seated, their laughter carrying across the water. They looked up as Lynn and Maddie approached, their expressions curious but welcoming.

"Ladies, this is Maddie Scott. The artist I told you about. She's the one responsible for those gorgeous paintings I just bought for the house." Lynn gestured to each woman in turn.

"Maddie, this is Kathy, Eileen, Susie, and Danielle. Between us, we've been summering in Ocean City for a combined total of about a hundred and fifty years."

"Don't do the math too carefully," the woman introduced as Kathy said dryly. "Some of us prefer to remain ageless."

Maddie found an empty spot on the cushioned bench. She'd agonized over what to wear, finally settling on white jeans and a flowy top she thought struck the right balance. No one commented, and the women shifted to make room for her, their smiles warm and open.

"So you're the one Lynn has been raving about," Danielle said, leaning forward with interest. Her dark hair was cut in a chic bob, and her jewelry was understated but clearly expensive. "She showed us photos of your work. That painting of the jetty is stunning."

"Thank you. That one took me months to get right."

"Art should take time," Eileen said. She had an effortless polish that spoke of prep schools and summers in Nantucket. "Anything worthwhile does."

A steward circled with a tray of champagne flutes, and Maddie accepted one gratefully. The first sip was cold and perfect, tiny bubbles dancing on her tongue.

"The captain will take us out past the inlet before sunset," Lynn announced, settling into her seat. "The dolphins have been particularly active this week."

"I saw them yesterday morning," Susie added. She was the quietest of the group so far. "A whole pod, right off the beach. The grandchildren were beside themselves."

The conversation flowed easily after that, moving from dolphins to family to the state of various beach houses and the ongoing struggle to find reliable help for summer entertaining. Maddie listened more than she spoke, absorbing the rhythms of their friendship, the shorthand that came from years of shared summers and holidays.

These women moved through life differently than she did.

They spoke casually about houses in multiple states, about winter trips to Palm Beach and spring weeks in Paris. Their problems were real enough but existed in another register altogether. Whose decorator had disappointed them. Which beach club was getting too crowded. Whether the new restaurant on Atlantic Avenue was worth the wait.

Maddie thought about the box of chocolates she'd brought —a twenty-dollar splurge that had felt generous at the time. She pictured her gallery, the rent she sometimes scrambled to make in the off-season, the used Honda she'd parked at the far end of the marina lot. These women probably spent more on a single dinner than she earned in a week. They had to know that. Which made her wonder why she was here at all.

And yet, she began to relax into the conversation. There was genuine warmth here, real friendship underneath the polish. When Kathy teased Eileen about her golf game, the laughter was inclusive, and Maddie laughed along.

Then Susie mentioned that her daughter was going through a difficult divorce.

"Oh, honey." Danielle reached over to squeeze Susie's hand. "How are you holding up?"

"It's been hard. The children are confused, and Jessica's a mess. She's staying with us for a few weeks while she figures things out."

"Well, at least she has you," Eileen said. She paused, swirling her glass. "Though I have to say, I never understood what she saw in that man. Remember the rehearsal dinner? His family."

"Oh God, the mother," Kathy agreed.

"He was always a bit rough around the edges," Lynn added. "And that polo shirt at the Yacht Club dinner."

The women exchanged knowing looks, and the mood changed. A ripple of discomfort passed through Maddie. They'd moved seamlessly from sympathy to scrutiny, their concern for Susie's daughter giving way to something sharper.

"Anyway," Susie said quietly, "she's better off."

"Of course she is." Danielle's voice was gentle again, the moment passed. "She'll land on her feet. Girls like her always do."

"Maddie, Lynn tells us you've lived in Ocean City year-round for several years now," Danielle said, turning the conversation toward her. "What's that like? We're always gone by Labor Day."

"It's quiet," Maddie said. "Which I love. The beaches feel like they belong to you again. The light in October is incredible—perfect for painting."

"How charming," Eileen said. "Like having your own private retreat."

"I've always wondered about the off-season," Kathy admitted. "What the town is like when we're not here."

"It's a different community. Smaller. Everyone knows everyone."

"That sounds lovely," Danielle said, though her tone suggested she found it anything but. "Though I don't know what I'd do without the club, the tennis, the social calendar. I'd go absolutely stir-crazy."

"Some of us need less stimulation than others," Lynn said lightly, and Maddie couldn't tell if it was meant as a defense or a gentle dig.

One of the crew came by to collect empty glasses, and Kathy held hers out without looking at him, continuing her conversation as if he weren't there. "Did I tell you about the new girl we hired to help with the house? Completely useless. I had to explain three times how to fold a fitted sheet."

"You can't find good help anymore," Eileen agreed. "We've gone through four housekeepers this year alone."

Maddie caught the crew member's expression—carefully neutral, professionally blank—and felt a twist of recognition. She'd worn that expression herself, years ago, waiting tables at a high-end restaurant in Philadelphia to pay for art supplies.

"The problem is they all want to be paid like professionals but work like amateurs," Kathy continued. She glanced at Maddie suddenly, as if remembering she was there. "Oh, but you probably handle everything yourself, don't you? In your little gallery?"

"I do, yes."

"See, that's the advantage of a simpler life. You don't have to rely on anyone."

Maddie smiled and said nothing. She wasn't sure if she'd just been complimented or condescended to.

The engine rumbled to life beneath them, and the yacht began to ease away from the dock. Maddie watched the marina recede, the rows of boats growing smaller, the shore transforming into a distant line of green and white.

"Come," Lynn said, rising from her seat. "Let me show you the rest of the boat before we settle in for the cruise."

The tour was impressive. The main salon featured leather furniture and a bar stocked with enough liquor to supply a small restaurant. The galley was spotless, fitted with professional-grade appliances. The master stateroom had a king-sized bed and its own bathroom with a rain shower and marble countertops.

"This is bigger than my first apartment," Maddie murmured, running her hand along the teak paneling.

Lynn laughed. "My husband insisted on every possible upgrade when we bought her. He's only been on board maybe a dozen times in five years, but he wanted it perfect anyway." A shadow crossed her face, there and gone. "Men and their toys."

They returned to the back deck as the yacht cleared the inlet and entered the open bay. The water stretched out in every direction, deep blue where the sun still reached it, darker in the shadows cast by the far shore. A light breeze carried the salt smell that Maddie associated with everything good about living here.

The conversation had turned during their absence. Eileen

was telling a story about a party she'd attended in the eighties, a minor celebrity and a mishap with a champagne fountain. The others were chiming in, adding details they remembered, correcting her on names and dates.

Maddie sipped her drink and tried to follow along, but the names meant nothing to her—people she'd never met, places she'd never been, a world that existed parallel to hers but never quite touched it. She laughed when the others laughed, a beat behind, not quite sure what was funny.

At some point, she caught Kathy's gaze drift down to her jeans, then back up with a tight, appraising smile. Heat rose to her cheeks—she was aware now that "casual" meant something different to these women than it did to her.

"There they are," Susie said suddenly, pointing.

A pod of dolphins had appeared off the starboard side, their dorsal fins cutting through the water in graceful arcs. The captain slowed the yacht, and everyone moved to the railing to watch. The dolphins seemed almost to be performing, leaping and diving, their sleek bodies catching the light.

"I never get tired of this," Lynn said softly, standing beside Maddie. "No matter how many times I see them."

"They're beautiful."

"They are." Lynn was quiet for a moment. "I'm glad you came today. I know this isn't your usual scene."

Maddie glanced at her, surprised by the directness. "Is it that obvious?"

"Not obvious, no. But I recognize the look. I married into this world. I wasn't born to it." Lynn smiled. "You learn to navigate it, eventually. Take what you need and leave the rest."

The dolphins moved on, their fins disappearing from view as the yacht continued on. The women returned to their seats, to fresh glasses of champagne and a new round of hors d'oeuvres. Maddie made herself join the conversation, laughing at their stories, offering a few of her own when prompted. She had no idea if the effort showed.

By the time the sun began its descent toward the horizon, painting the sky in shades of pink and gold, Maddie didn't know what to make of the evening. These women were charming, certainly. Interesting, even. They seemed truly interested in her work. But beneath the charm, she sensed something else—an offhand cruelty that surfaced in small moments and then vanished again, quick as a knife.

"We should do this again," Kathy said as the yacht turned back toward the marina. "Maddie, you'll come to brunch at my place next week? Chef Antonio is flying in from New York—he does this incredible spread. Very intimate, just us girls."

"That sounds wonderful," Maddie said, though she only half believed it.

"Wednesday at eleven. I'll have my assistant send the address."

The marina came into view, the boats in their slips gilded by the last of the evening sun. As the crew prepared to dock, Maddie felt the strange sensation of returning from somewhere very far away, even though she'd never been more than a few miles from shore.

"Thank you for inviting me," she said to Lynn as the gangway was secured. "This was lovely."

"It was, wasn't it?" Lynn squeezed her hand. "I'll make sure you get the details about Kathy's brunch."

Maddie stepped off the yacht and onto the solid planks of the dock. Behind her, the women's voices rose in a final chorus of goodbyes. She turned to wave, and Lynn blew her a kiss from the deck.

Walking back down the pier, Maddie tried to process the evening. The champagne. The dolphins. The breezy talk of houses and clubs and winters in sunnier places. The way they'd dissected Susie's son-in-law, the dismissiveness toward the crew, that look Kathy had given her jeans.

Parts of it had been fun, actually. But something about the evening left her unsettled.

She paused and looked over her shoulder. *The Good Life* glowed in the fading light, the women's laughter drifting across the marina. They were probably pouring one more drink, making plans for the week ahead, moving through their summer with the confidence of people who belonged exactly where they were.

Maddie belonged on the beach, in her gallery, in front of a canvas with a brush in her hand. She belonged in Ocean City year-round, watching storms roll in and painting the light that came after. This other world was beautiful to visit, but she couldn't shake the feeling that she was being invited to play a part in someone else's story.

CHAPTER SEVEN

The spa in Strathmere occupied a renovated beach cottage on a quiet stretch of road, its cedar shingles weathered to a soft gray that blended with the dunes behind it. A hand-painted sign reading Seagrass Wellness hung from a post near the gravel parking lot, swaying gently in the offshore breeze. Claire had found the place online after deciding that what she needed after her string of dating disasters wasn't another app, another profile, another dinner across from a man who wanted to tell her about his morning routine. What she needed was someone to work out the knots in her shoulders and not say a single word to her for an hour.

She pushed through the front door and was immediately hit with the scent of eucalyptus, rosemary and mint. The reception area was small but thoughtfully decorated: driftwood accents, sea-glass votives on the windowsill, a bubbling fountain in the corner that created a steady, calming white noise. A young woman with her hair in a neat bun looked up from behind the desk.

"Claire?"

"That's me."

"Perfect. We have you down for the ninety-minute deep

tissue. You're a few minutes early, so feel free to have a seat. Jessica will be with you shortly."

Claire settled into one of the oversized armchairs in the waiting area, grateful for the stillness. Through the windows, she could see the bay stretching out behind the building, its surface rippled by the morning breeze. A handful of boats dotted the water in the distance. She pulled out her phone, silenced it, and dropped it back into her purse. The whole point of coming here was to disconnect.

The front door opened, and Claire's attention shifted out of habit.

The man who walked in had to duck slightly to clear the frame. He was tall, over six feet, with broad shoulders that tested the seams of his plain gray T-shirt. His build suggested someone who had spent years doing something physical. His face was handsome in an unpolished way, strong jaw covered by a neatly trimmed beard, deep-set eyes, the kind of features that looked like they'd been carved rather than assembled. His hair was cropped short and starting to show gray at the temples, the beard following suit.

He approached the desk, gave his name in a low voice Claire couldn't quite catch, and was directed to the same waiting area.

He looked over as he took the chair across from her. He nodded. She nodded back. A polite acknowledgment between strangers about to spend the next hour and a half being kneaded by professionals.

Claire picked up one of the magazines from the side table, a year-old issue about gourmet cooking, and pretended to read it. But something nagged at her. She glanced up again, studying him from behind the pages.

She knew him from somewhere. She was sure of it.

The recognition was maddening in its vagueness. Not a friend of a friend, not someone from the neighborhood. Somewhere else entirely. A face she'd seen but couldn't place, like a word stuck on the tip of her tongue.

He must have felt her looking, because he glanced over and raised an eyebrow, the corner of his mouth twitching upward.

"Sorry," Claire said, lowering the magazine. "You just look really familiar. Did you go to Temple? In Philly?"

He laughed, a surprised sound that seemed to catch him off guard. "Can't say I did."

"Huh. I could have sworn..." She trailed off. "Never mind. It's going to bug me all day now."

Before he could respond, a door opened and a woman in scrubs appeared. "Claire? I'm Jessica. Ready to get started?"

Claire gathered her purse and stood. "Good luck," she said to the man, though she wasn't sure why.

He smiled. "You too."

* * *

The massage room was dim and quiet, a carefully constructed stillness that made Claire's shoulders drop three inches the moment she lay face-down on the table. Jessica had skilled hands and, thankfully, didn't seem inclined toward small talk. She worked in silence, finding knots Claire hadn't known she was carrying and methodically dismantling them.

Claire let her mind drift. The kids were due back from Brian's in a week. She'd filled the time with work and errands and exactly two disastrous attempts at dating, but the emptiness remained underneath it all, waiting for her in the spaces between activities.

Maybe that was okay. Maybe she needed to sit with the emptiness for a while instead of trying to fill it with bourbon-drinking complainers and men who posted her photo on social media before the first date was over.

Jessica was working on her lower back when Claire heard it.

Laughter. Faint at first, muffled by the wall between the treatment rooms. Then louder. Then louder still.

It was a man's laugh, uncontrolled and helpless—the sound of someone being tickled against their will.

"Sorry," Jessica said, pausing her movements. "That's the room next door. First-time client, I think."

The laughter continued, building in waves. Claire could hear a man's voice underneath it, probably the massage therapist, saying something that only made the laughter worse.

"What's going on over there?" Claire asked, fighting a smile. "Telling jokes during the massage?"

"I've had clients like that. Probably just ticklish."

Claire pressed her face into the massage table's headrest and felt her own laughter building. She tried to suppress it, tried to maintain the Zen calm she'd been cultivating for the past forty minutes, but the absurdity of the moment was too much. A snort escaped her.

Through the wall, the man's laughter hit a new peak, followed by what sounded like an apology. The therapist's voice again. More laughter.

"Should we maybe play some music?" Jessica suggested.

"No," Claire managed. "This is actually better."

By the time the session ended, Claire's cheeks hurt from suppressed giggles. She felt lighter than she had in weeks, though whether that was from the massage or the unexpected comedy show, she couldn't say.

She changed back into her clothes and made her way to the reception desk to pay. The man from the waiting room emerged from the hallway at the same moment, his face still flushed.

He spotted her and stopped walking.

"You heard that," he said.

"I think they heard it in Cape May."

He covered his face with one hand. "This is extremely embarrassing."

"Don't worry about it. Could have happened to anyone."

"It really couldn't have." He dropped his hand with a rueful smile. "I haven't had a massage in years. Forgot that I'm..." He gestured vaguely. "Like that."

The receptionist looked between them with barely concealed amusement. "Ready to check out?"

"Please," Claire said, stepping forward and handing over her credit card. She signed the receipt quickly, aware of him waiting behind her, still radiating embarrassment.

"Well," she said, tucking her card back into her purse, "at least it made for an entertaining morning."

He laughed, a short, self-deprecating sound. "Glad someone enjoyed it."

She headed for the door, glancing back once. He was approaching the desk now, pulling out his wallet. The strong jaw, the serious eyes that had just been crinkling with involuntary laughter. It would come to her eventually. It always did.

Outside, the late morning had brightened into a beautiful day, the bay sparkling beyond the dunes. Claire walked to her car, already thinking about what to do with the hours ahead. A book, maybe. A drink somewhere quiet. An afternoon that didn't require anything from her except showing up.

* * *

The Deauville Inn sat on the bay side of Strathmere, a waterfront institution that had been serving drinks and seafood for decades. Claire walked past the dining room and out to the outdoor bar. She claimed a stool at the long wooden counter. The bay was somewhere beyond the crowded tables and umbrellas—she could hear boats motoring past, catch glimpses of water between the gaps in the crowd.

It wasn't far from the spa, and something about the day made her want to extend it rather than head straight home. She retrieved the book she'd left in her car, a novel she'd been meaning to finish for three weeks. The binding was cracked from being stuffed into beach bags and abandoned on nightstands, and she wasn't entirely sure she remembered what was happening in the plot. But it gave her hands something to do and her eyes somewhere to look besides her phone.

The bartender came over, and she ordered an orange crush and a burger.

The bar was about half full. A couple in their sixties occupied the far end, clearly regulars based on their easy rapport with the bartender. The Phillies game played on the TV mounted above the liquor bottles, and a few people glanced up at it between conversations. A group of younger women clustered around a high-top table nearby, their laughter punctuating the ambient noise. Claire had positioned herself between these poles, visible enough to not seem like she was hiding, but far enough from both groups to maintain her solitude.

She was two chapters in, her burger half-eaten, when she felt it. A shift in the energy around her. The bartender's posture changing slightly. The couple at the end of the bar glancing toward someone approaching.

Claire looked up.

The man from the spa was walking toward the bar, scanning for an open seat. He was unmistakable. The height. The shoulders. That face.

He must have found what he was looking for, because he took a stool two seats down from Claire without seeming to notice her.

"What can I get you?" the bartender asked.

"Beer. Whatever you have on tap that's local."

The bartender poured it and set it in front of him. He took a long drink, set the glass down, and then reached into the messenger bag he'd been carrying.

He pulled out a book.

Claire stared. Here was a grown man, easily six-four, sitting at a bar in the middle of the day with a paperback in hand. He opened it to a bookmarked page and started reading, apparently oblivious to everything around him.

She lasted about thirty seconds.

"Weren't you just at Seagrass Wellness?"

His head came up. For a moment, confusion clouded his features. Then recognition dawned, and he winced.

"The tickle room," he said. "I was hoping you wouldn't recognize me. Or at least pretend not to."

Claire smiled. "Sorry. Hard to forget."

He shook his head, but he was grinning. "Can't blame you. Are you following me, or is this a coincidence?"

"Pure coincidence."

"Twice in one day. What are the odds?"

"In Strathmere? Probably higher than you'd think." Claire picked up her glass. "What are you reading?"

He held up the cover. It was a biography of some historical figure she vaguely recognized but couldn't identify. "Light beach reading," he said dryly.

"Very light. I'm impressed you can lift it."

He laughed, that same easy sound from the spa, and Claire found herself relaxing. This was nice. Simple. Just two people at a bar, exchanging words without the weight of expectation that came with dating apps and planned encounters.

"I'm Claire, by the way."

"Troy." He raised his beer glass slightly in acknowledgment. "Nice to officially meet you. Under less embarrassing circumstances."

Claire noticed a woman at a nearby table glance over at them, then lean toward her companion and whisper something.

He nodded toward her book. "What about you? What are you reading?"

She held it up. A novel with a beach scene on the cover, waves and sand and a woman walking toward an uncertain horizon. "Actual light beach reading. Don't judge me."

"No judgment here. I've been known to binge reality television when no one's watching."

"Which shows?"

"I'm not telling you that. We just met."

"Fair." Claire took another sip of her drink. "So. Troy. What brings you to the area?"

The lightness in his expression faded briefly, then steadied. "Needed some time away. A place to think."

"Thinking about anything specific?"

He turned his beer glass slowly on the bar, watching the condensation leave trails on the wood. "What comes next, mostly. The work part of my life is fine. It's everything else that's up in the air."

Claire recognized the sentiment. "I know that feeling."

"Yeah?"

"I moved here last month. My husband and I were supposed to come together, but his job offer fell through at the last minute. He decided not to come. I decided to come anyway." She said it matter-of-factly, the way she'd learned to say it after weeks of practice. "Turns out he had someone waiting in the wings back home, so it worked out for everyone. We're separated now."

"That took guts," he said. "Moving anyway."

"Or maybe I just didn't want to let him take this from me too."

"How's that working out?"

"Some days are better than others. I've got my kids, my sister's nearby, my parents. I'm trying to remember who I am when I'm not someone's wife." She paused. "The dating part's been less successful."

Troy grimaced. "Bad experiences?"

"Let's just say I've met some interesting characters. One guy complained about everything from the drive to the music to his bourbon. Another one researched my entire online history before we even met. Knew which restaurant reviews I'd left."

"That's..." He exhaled. "That's a lot."

"Two strikes was enough. I'm taking a break from all that."

He chuckled, and Claire felt something ease in her chest. He was grounding to be around. Conversation felt effortless in a way it hadn't with anyone in a long time.

"So your sister's in Ocean City too?"

"She runs a couple of places there. Chipper's, it's a breakfast spot. And Romano's, this little vintage shop. Family businesses. I help out sometimes when she needs an extra hand." She set her glass down. "What about you? Anyone waiting for you back home?"

A shadow passed over his face. "Not anymore. We separated about six months ago. I was on the road a lot for work, and I thought she was fine with it. She was more than fine, actually. She'd found someone to keep her company while I was gone."

"I'm sorry."

"Don't be. I missed the signs because I wasn't paying attention. That's on me." He lifted the beer to his lips. "Anyway. Ancient history now."

They sat with that for a moment, the shared understanding of people who'd been through similar things. The bartender drifted by, and Claire ordered another orange crush.

"Can I ask you something?" Claire said.

"Shoot."

"This is going to sound crazy, but I cannot figure out where I know you from. It's been driving me nuts all day."

"I get that a lot."

"You do?"

"Hazard of the former job." He ran a thumb along the rim of his glass. "You really don't know, do you?"

"Know what?"

He studied her for a moment, a small smile playing at the

corners of his mouth. "Nothing. Just surprised, is all. Most people figure it out faster."

"Figure what out?"

"Doesn't matter." He picked up his book, then set it down again. "I like that you don't know. It's refreshing."

Claire frowned. "You're being very cryptic."

"Am I? Sorry. Old habit." He signaled the bartender for another beer. "Tell me more about starting over. What's the hardest part?"

She let him change the subject, even though the mystery of his identity continued to nag at her. There would be time to figure it out later. Right now, she was enjoying this too much to push.

"The hardest part is remembering I get to decide things now," she said. "For twenty years, every choice was filtered through someone else. What he wanted, what worked for the family, what kept the peace. Now I can do whatever I want, and half the time I don't even know what that is."

"So what do you do?"

"That's what I'm still figuring out. Sometimes I take walks on the beach. Sometimes I sit at bars and read books I'm never going to finish." She gestured around them. "Sometimes I run into strangers who can't handle a massage and end up having actual conversations."

"Sounds like a solid strategy."

"It's a work in progress."

The bartender brought Troy's beer, and he raised it slightly in Claire's direction. "To works in progress."

She clinked her glass against his bottle. "To works in progress."

They talked for hours, the afternoon slipping past unnoticed. Ocean City and what made it different from other shore towns. The strange relief of being somewhere no one knew your history. Books and bad television and the specific pleasure of eating alone at a bar without anyone expecting you to make conversation.

At no point did Troy offer his phone number. At no point did Claire ask for it. There was an unspoken understanding between them that this was what it was, a chance encounter between two people at a particular moment in their lives, valuable precisely because it didn't have to become anything more.

When Claire finally checked her watch, it was nearly five. "I should go," she said, reaching for her purse.

"Me too." Troy closed his book, marking his place with a receipt from the bar. "This was nice. Really nice."

"It was." Claire stood, gathering her things. "Thanks for keeping me company."

"Thanks for not holding the spa thing against me."

She laughed. "I make no promises about future encounters."

"Fair enough."

They walked out together into the late-afternoon air. The bay glittered beyond the docks, a few boats making their way back toward the marina. Somewhere in the distance, an engine hummed.

"Take care of yourself, Claire," Troy said.

"You too, Troy. Good luck with the figuring-things-out part."

"Same to you."

He walked toward the parking lot, and she watched him go, still trying to place that face. Maybe it would hit her in the middle of the night. Maybe next week. The not-knowing was frustrating and somehow also part of the appeal.

* * *

The kayaks scraped against sand as Lauren and Matt pulled them onto the shore of the hidden cove. The afternoon had softened into early evening, late sun slanting across the sea-glass-strewn beach, the air carrying that distinct quality of June when the day seemed reluctant to end.

"Look at this," Matt said, crouching near the waterline. A new deposit had appeared since their last visit, a fresh layer of tumbled glass catching what light remained. "The tide's been busy."

Lauren knelt beside him, running her fingers through the pieces. Greens and browns, mostly, but here and there flashes of blue, a streak of amber. The cove never stopped giving. Each visit revealed something new, as if the ocean had been saving these treasures for decades, waiting for someone to finally notice.

They'd brought larger bags this time, and a proper collection container that wouldn't puncture. The plan was to fill what they could carry and paddle back before the tide turned.

"Should we see if the camper is still there?" Lauren asked, glancing toward the dunes.

"Let's collect first," Matt said. "Give them space if they want it."

They spread out across the beach, falling into step, no discussion needed. Matt gravitated toward the rocks at the cove's edge, where larger pieces tended to accumulate in the crevices. Lauren worked the main stretch of shore, methodically scanning, selecting, depositing.

Twenty minutes in, her bag was already heavy. She'd found a red piece the size of her thumbnail, genuinely red, not the orange-tinged amber that sometimes passed for it. Red glass was the rarest, and this piece was a beauty.

"Matt," she called, holding it up. "Look."

He jogged over, examined it, eyebrows rising. "That's a good one."

"I know." She tucked it carefully into a side pocket, separate from the rest. Some pieces deserved their own space.

They kept working as the light slowly changed. The cove took on an amber cast, then gold, then something closer to rose. Lauren checked her watch. Still time. They had at least an hour before they'd need to leave.

That was when she heard the voice.

"You two are getting good at this."

Lauren spun. A woman stood at the edge of the beach grass, watching them with an expression of bemused curiosity. She was maybe forty, lean and tanned in the way of people who spent most of their time outdoors. Her hair was sun-bleached and pulled back in a ponytail, and she wore quick-dry athletic clothes that suggested serious outdoor pursuits.

"I saw you here the other day," the woman added, stepping onto the beach. "Figured if you came back, I'd say hello."

Matt moved to Lauren's side, instinctively protective. "You're the one with the tent."

"Guilty." The woman extended her hand. "I'm Rae. Short for Rachel, but nobody's called me that since high school."

Lauren shook it. "Lauren. This is Matt."

"How long have you been here?" Lauren asked.

"A couple weeks, give or take. I'm a freediver. I was investigating a wreck offshore when I stumbled onto this place." Rae gestured around the cove. "Thought I'd camp for a few days, do some documentation. Few days turned into a couple weeks. You know how it goes."

"What wreck?" Matt asked.

Rae's eyes lit up with the particular enthusiasm of someone who'd been sitting on a story and was finally being asked to tell it. "That's where it gets interesting. Want to see something?"

She led them through the dunes to her camp, which looked much as it had on their previous visit. The tent. The fire pit. The solar panel and the careful organization. But Rae had clearly been busy—a waterproof notebook sat open on the folding table, a camera with a serious lens beside it. Maps were now pinned to a board, marked with circles and annotations.

And the mason jars. Dozens of them now, far more than before, each filled with sorted sea glass.

"The wreck is about a quarter mile offshore—I paddle out in my inflatable," Rae said, pulling out one of the maps. "Went down in 1923, a cargo vessel called the *Esther Pearl*. She was carrying machine parts and textiles, nothing exciting. Hit a sandbar in a storm and broke apart."

Lauren listened, curious where this was heading. Matt had drifted over to study the maps.

"I've been diving that wreck for years. Know every inch of her. When I found this cove and saw all the glass, my first assumption was that it was debris from the ship. Some of those old vessels carried bottles, glassware, that kind of thing." Rae pulled out one of the mason jars, held it up to what light filtered through the trees. "But then I started looking closer."

Lauren leaned in.

"Wrong type of glass entirely." Rae set the jar down and picked up her notebook, flipping to a page covered in notes. "The *Esther Pearl* wasn't carrying glassware. I checked the manifest—machine parts and textiles, nothing else. This glass came from somewhere else."

Lauren exchanged a glance with Matt. They'd wondered about the source. Now someone was offering answers.

"So where's it coming from?" Matt asked.

Rae grinned. "I did some digging. Talked to some historians, some old-timers, dug through archives at the historical society. Turns out, in the 1920s and 30s, there was a dump site just offshore. Maybe a hundred yards out."

"A dump site?"

"Prohibition era. When alcohol was illegal, people still drank. They just did it secretly. And when you're running illegal booze, you accumulate a lot of bottles. Bottles you can't exactly dispose of through normal channels." Rae pointed toward the mouth of the cove. "They used to dump them offshore, late at night. Weighted crates full of empty whiskey bottles, wine bottles, medicine bottles that may or may not have contained 'medicine.'" She made air quotes. "Thousands and thousands of bottles, tossed into the ocean over more than a decade."

Lauren felt her understanding of the cove shift. Not just random bottles tossed overboard over the years. A deliberate dump site, a century-old secret, washing ashore at last.

"The nor'easters this winter," Rae continued. "They shifted the sand, opened up that channel you've been using. But they also disturbed the dump site. Sent decades of buried glass back into circulation." She spread her arms to encompass the beach. "All of this? It's Prohibition history. Every piece has a story."

"That's incredible," Matt said.

"It's better than incredible. It's a genuine archaeological find." Rae's voice dropped slightly, taking on a more serious tone. "Which is why I've been documenting everything. Taking samples, photographing locations, mapping the distribution patterns. This isn't just valuable glass. It's evidence of how an entire community operated during one of the strangest periods in American history."

Lauren looked around the cove with new eyes. The beach wasn't just a treasure trove. It was a time capsule.

"Are you going to publish something?" she asked. "Report it to someone?"

"Eventually. I'm still gathering data. And honestly?" Rae laughed, shaking her head. "I've been sitting on this alone. Having people to actually talk to about it is kind of intoxicating."

She seemed to realize what she'd said and blushed slightly. "Sorry. I get excited about this stuff."

"Don't apologize," Lauren said. "This is fascinating."

They spent the next hour deep in conversation. Rae showed them her documentation, the photographs she'd taken of particularly significant pieces, the patterns she'd identified in the distribution. She explained how bottle colors indicated time periods, manufacturers, purposes. The cobalt blue came from medicine bottles, many of them carrying laudanum or other "tonics" that were really just vehicles for alcohol. The red was rarer—expensive decorative tableware, ships' lanterns, the occasional warning light.

The evening settled in around them, but Lauren barely noticed. This was exactly the rabbit hole she loved falling into, the discovery that there was always more to learn, more to understand.

It was Matt who checked his watch and went pale.

"Lauren."

"What?"

"It's seven forty-five."

The words took a moment to register. Then she understood. The tide. The channel. The window they'd planned to use had closed while they were talking.

"Oh no."

Rae looked between them. "What's wrong?"

"We were supposed to leave before the tide came back in. The channel, it's only passable at low tide."

"And now it's not?"

Matt shook his head. "Those overhangs we ducked under—there won't be any clearance now. The rocks will be underwater, but not deep enough to paddle over. We'd be pinned against the ceiling."

Lauren felt a flutter of panic, then forced herself to think logically. Rae had supplies. They had shelter options. This wasn't a crisis, just an inconvenience.

"Next low tide would be around seven-thirty or eight tomorrow morning," Rae said, consulting her charts. "You're stuck here until then." She looked apologetic. "Sorry—I've got a little inflatable I paddle around the point, but it barely holds me. Never thought about the channel timing." She moved to the fire pit and crouched down, arranging kindling. "You two hungry? I've got enough for three if you don't mind camp food."

Matt put his arm around Lauren's shoulders. "I guess we're having an adventure. Camp food sounds perfect."

Matt helped Rae gather driftwood from the edge of the dunes while Lauren watched the fire catch and grow. The wood crackled and popped, sending sparks spiraling up into the darkening sky. Soon flames were licking steadily at the logs, throwing warm light across the sand.

Rae set a pot of water on the camp stove to boil while the fire built up. "Rice and beans okay? There's some dried vegetables I can throw in."

"Sounds perfect," Lauren said, and meant it.

They ate cross-legged around the fire, balancing camp bowls on their knees. The food was simple—rice and beans with rehydrated peppers and onions—but after a day of paddling and collecting, it tasted better than it had any right to. The fire snapped and hissed. Waves rolled against the shore in the darkness beyond. Lauren hadn't felt this far from everything in ages.

Lauren hesitated then decided to just say it. "We should probably mention—we've been collecting too. The sea glass. We didn't know anyone else was here at first."

Rae shrugged, unbothered. "I noticed. Hard to miss the bags." She poked at the fire with a stick. "Doesn't matter to me. I'm not here to sell the stuff—I'm here to document it. The history, the story, that's what I care about." She nodded toward the dark beach. "Besides, there's more glass in this cove than the three of us could collect in a lifetime. The ocean keeps bringing more."

"You're not worried about people finding out? Coming here and picking it clean?"

"I go back and forth on it. There's something to be said for keeping a place like this quiet. But eventually someone else will stumble on it." Rae smiled. "And you two seem like you get it."

Rae leaned back in her camp chair. "There's a tarp if you want to set up under it. Keeps the dew off."

Lauren glanced at Matt. He met her eyes. Some unspoken communication passed between them.

"Actually," Lauren said, "would it be crazy if we just slept on the beach?"

Rae considered this. "Not crazy at all. There's a sandy stretch near the rocks that's sheltered from the breeze. I can loan you a blanket."

"When's the last time we got to do something like this?" Matt asked Lauren. "Just sleep outside, with nothing between us and the sky?"

She couldn't remember. Maybe not ever—not like this, anyway.

"Let's do it," she said.

They dragged their kayaks all the way up the beach, well above where the high tide would reach. Rae handed them a blanket to lie on and showed them the spot she'd mentioned near the rocks.

As the last light faded, Lauren lay back on the blanket and watched the stars emerge. First one, then another, then suddenly dozens, then hundreds, pricking through the darkness like holes in a curtain. The Milky Way stretched overhead, visible in a way it never was in the city, never was anywhere with lights and noise and the constant hum of civilization.

Matt lay beside her, his hand finding hers.

"I've never seen anything like this," he murmured.

"Neither have I."

Rae had retreated to her tent, giving them privacy, but Lauren could see the faint glow of a headlamp through the fabric. She was probably documenting something, adding to her meticulous records.

"What do you think she's going to do with all of it?" Matt asked. "The research, I mean."

"I don't know. Write a paper? Contact a museum?" A satellite traversed the sky, a tiny point of light moving steadily among the stationary stars. "It feels strange to think about this place going public."

"Strange how?"

"Because once it's public, this place changes. People will come. The glass will disappear. The cove will become just another attraction." She squeezed his hand. "Right now it's still a secret. Ours and hers. I know that can't last, but it feels special."

"It does."

They stayed like that for a while, listening to the rhythm of the waves, the occasional rustle of wind through the dune grass. Somewhere out in the darkness, fish jumped. Crabs scuttled across the sand. The cove went about its nocturnal business, oblivious to the humans in its midst.

CHAPTER EIGHT

The address Lynn had forwarded led Maddie out of Ocean City entirely, south through Avalon and into Stone Harbor. She'd had reservations after the yacht—the evening had left her unsettled—but Lynn's follow-up text had been persuasive. The girls loved meeting you. Kathy especially wants to talk about commissioning something for her place. A commission from someone like Kathy could lead to three more. Maddie was a working artist; she couldn't afford to be precious about where the work came from.

The driveway to Kathy's place was easy to miss—just a break in a tall hedge with a small brass number on a stone pillar. Maddie turned through the open iron gate and followed a crushed-shell driveway that wound through grounds land-scaped to look effortlessly natural. Specimen trees dotted mani-cured lawns. A gardener on a riding mower worked a stretch of grass in the distance. The drive curved past a guest cottage before the main house finally revealed itself.

It sprawled across the waterfront, all glass and silvered cedar, three stories that seemed to unfold in every direction. A four-car garage sat to one side. A pool house anchored the other. The property had to take up half the block—an almost unthinkable footprint even for Stone Harbor. A fountain burbled in the circular drive, which was large enough to accommodate half a dozen cars without crowding.

She parked her Honda between a black Range Rover and a silver Porsche, suddenly conscious of the coffee stain on her passenger seat and the beach towel crumpled in the back. On the yacht, everything had felt contained, manageable. Here, surrounded by all this curated perfection, she was exposed.

A woman in a black polo shirt and khaki pants appeared at the side of the house, carrying a tray of glasses toward what Maddie assumed was the kitchen door. The woman glanced at Maddie, did a quick scan of her outfit, and gestured with her chin.

"Caterers are setting up around back. You can go through the service entrance."

Maddie hesitated. "Oh. No, I'm not—I'm a guest."

The woman's expression shifted, what might have been embarrassment crossing her features before it smoothed into professional neutrality. "Of course. I'm sorry. The front door's just there." She nodded toward it and hurried away before Maddie could respond.

It was a small thing. A reasonable mistake, probably. Maddie was wearing shorts and a tank top, nothing that screamed money or social standing. But the quickness of the assumption, the way the woman had scanned her and made a judgment in half a second, said plenty about the world she was walking into. She stood in the driveway, the fountain splashing behind her, wondering if this was the universe sending her a message.

She thought about getting back in her car. Driving home. Texting Lynn some excuse about a migraine or a gallery emergency. But she'd driven all the way out here, and backing out now seemed ridiculous. She adjusted the strap of her purse and headed for the front door.

Inside, the house was even more impressive. Soaring ceilings, furniture that managed to be both minimalist and clearly expensive. Through the floor-to-ceiling windows, the bay spread out like hammered silver. A dock extended from the property's edge, a white speedboat tied at its end. Maddie followed the sound of voices to a living room where Kathy, Lynn, Eileen, Susie, and Danielle were already gathered, along with a woman Maddie didn't recognize.

"There she is!" Kathy swept toward her with a mimosa extended like an offering. "Maddie, welcome. You found us."

"Beautiful home," Maddie said, accepting the mimosa.

"Thank you. It was a nightmare to build, but worth every headache." Kathy steered her toward the others. "You remember everyone from the boat. And this is Vivian."

Vivian was perhaps sixty, with silver hair cut in a severe bob and jewelry that looked like it belonged in a museum. She gave Maddie a cool once-over and offered a brief, appraising smile.

"So you're the artist Lynn discovered." Vivian's tone made it sound like a species classification.

"That's me."

"How charming. Lynn has such a talent for finding interesting people."

Before Maddie could decide if that was a compliment, a young woman in the same black polo appeared at the edge of the room, waiting to be acknowledged. Kathy didn't turn around.

"The pastries should be out by now," she said, still facing the women.

"Yes, ma'am. Chef wanted me to let you know the mini quiches will be another few minutes."

"That's fine." A wave of dismissal, not even a glance. The young woman retreated silently.

They settled into conversation that reminded her of the yacht. Tennis and travel, children and grandchildren, the ongoing renovation of someone's kitchen that had stretched into its eighth month. Maddie listened more than she spoke, sipping her mimosa and studying the room. The mini quiches arrived eventually, passed around on a silver tray, and Maddie took one to be polite.

"Oh, Maddie," Kathy said suddenly, as if just remembering. "I wanted to ask you about that commission. I'm redoing my bedroom and I need something for over the bed. Abstract, soft colors, maybe some gold leaf. Something that ties the room together."

Maddie blinked. "Oh—I don't really do abstract work."

"But you could adapt, couldn't you? Something impressionistic, a bit looser than your usual style?" Kathy glanced at Vivian. "I saw the most gorgeous piece at a gallery in Palm Beach. Very modern, very now."

"Sounds lovely," Vivian said.

"We can discuss the details later." Kathy patted Maddie's arm. "I'll have my decorator send you the fabric swatches so you can match the colors exactly."

Maddie opened her mouth to explain that wasn't how her work functioned, but Kathy had already moved on to complimenting Eileen's bracelet. The commission, apparently, was settled.

A server came through with another tray of pastries. Vivian took one without acknowledging the woman holding the tray, continuing her story about a disastrous dinner party without so much as a pause. The server stood there, waiting, invisible.

"That's fine, that's fine," Kathy finally said, waving her away. Then, turning back: "I've told them a hundred times not to interrupt when we're talking."

The server retreated. Maddie watched her go, noting how carefully she kept her face blank.

A clatter came from somewhere near the kitchen, followed by a sharp voice. Kathy excused herself and disappeared down the hall. Through the doorway, Maddie could hear her laying into someone.

"This is the second time this month. Do you have any idea what those glasses cost? If you can't carry a tray without dropping it, I'll find someone who can."

A muffled apology, too soft to make out.

"Sorry doesn't replace Waterford crystal. Just—get this cleaned up. And stay out of sight until you do."

Kathy returned to the group, her face smoothing back into pleasant hostess mode as if nothing had happened.

"Maddie, we should have you do a little sketch of us," Kathy said, gesturing at the women around her. "You know, while we're all together. A memento of the afternoon."

Her smile froze. "A sketch?"

"Nothing elaborate. Just something quick. You have such a gift." Eileen looked around. "Wouldn't that be fun? A Maddie Scott original, right here in Kathy's living room."

"Oh, I love that idea," Danielle said. "Like having our own portrait artist."

"I appreciate that, but portraits aren't my thing," Maddie said, keeping her voice pleasant. "My work is seascapes, landscapes. I wouldn't know where to begin with faces."

Eileen waved a hand dismissively. "Oh, I'm sure you're being modest. An artist is an artist."

"It's actually quite different. The techniques, the approach—"

"We don't need anything fancy," Kathy cut in. "Just a fun little doodle. Surely you can manage that."

Heat rose to her cheeks. A fun little doodle. As if years of developing her craft were interchangeable party tricks.

"I'd really rather not," she said. "I wouldn't want to disappoint you with something outside my skill set."

An awkward silence settled over the room. Eileen's smile went rigid. Kathy exchanged a glance with Vivian that Maddie couldn't quite read.

"Well," Vivian said, her tone light but carrying an edge, "I suppose we can't all be versatile."

Lynn jumped in quickly. "Maddie's being professional. You wouldn't ask a heart surgeon to set a broken bone."

"It's hardly the same thing," Kathy murmured, but she let the subject drop. A beat passed, and then she pivoted. "That painting Lynn bought," she said. "The one of the boardwalk in winter? She showed it to me last week. Quite good."

"It really is lovely," Susie agreed.

"And so reasonably priced." Kathy glanced at Maddie. "Really, you should be charging twice as much. Three times, even. Though of course we won't complain."

Everyone laughed.

Reasonably priced. Maddie said nothing. She'd heard this before—customers who thought they were being kind by telling her she undervalued her work, never realizing how it sounded. Like her art was a bargain bin find. A steal. Something they were lucky to snap up before she figured out what it was really worth.

"I price my work where I think it should be," she said.

"That's so refreshing," Vivian said. "Most artists these days are so pretentious about money. Acting like they're doing you a favor by letting you buy their work."

"Maddie's not like that," Lynn said. "She's very down to earth."

Down to earth. Maddie reached for her glass.

Without breaking from the conversation, Kathy snapped her fingers toward the doorway. A young man appeared— barely out of high school, acne still visible along his jaw. He refilled her mimosa in silence.

"Not so much," Kathy said, not looking at him. "Half a glass. Do I need to do everything myself?"

The young man murmured an apology and adjusted the pour. Kathy's eyes never left the conversation.

"And tell whoever's running the kitchen that the mini

quiches were lukewarm. Lukewarm. I'm not paying premium prices for lukewarm food."

"Yes, ma'am."

He disappeared, and Kathy turned back as if nothing had happened. "You just can't find reliable help anymore. We've been through three different catering companies this summer."

"It's the same everywhere," Eileen agreed. "Nobody wants to work."

Maddie thought about the woman outside who had mistaken her for a caterer. The young man who had just been scolded for the pour. Whoever had been told to stay out of sight after dropping a glass. All of them moving through this house like ghosts, visible only when something went wrong.

"Excuse me," she said when the conversation moved on. "I need to use the restroom."

"Down the hall, second door on the left," Kathy said, her attention already back on Vivian.

Maddie made her way through the house, grateful for the reprieve. The bathroom was larger than her gallery's back room, all marble and brass fixtures and towels that looked like they'd never been used. She closed the door behind her.

The clasp on her bracelet had been catching all morning. She slipped it off and worked the tiny mechanism with her fingernail. It was a simple silver chain with a small shell charm—nothing expensive, but her grandmother had given it to her the summer before she died. Maddie had worn it almost every day since.

She got the clasp working again and set the bracelet on the marble counter, then leaned against the sink and stared at her reflection.

What was she doing here?

The question had been building since the yacht, growing louder with each interaction. How they'd dismissed her expertise like it was stubbornness. How they treated the staff like furniture. There was something in the way they looked at her, talked about her, that made her wonder if she was being collected rather than included.

She gripped the edge of the sink, took a breath, and stepped back into the hallway.

That was when she heard it.

Voices from around the corner, low but not quite low enough.

"—doing wonderfully, though. Credit to Lynn for bringing her along."

"Oh, Lynn always has a project." Vivian's distinctive voice. "Remember the potter from Stone Harbor a few years back?"

"That's different. The potter was actually talented."

"Maddie's talented," Eileen said. "In a certain way. Very commercial. The kind of thing you'd find at a street fair."

A ripple of laughter.

"Did you see the car she drove up in?" Vivian again. "I thought it was one of the caterers."

More laughter.

"I just hope Lynn knows what she's doing. These artist types can be so unpredictable. And needy. Give them an inch and they start expecting invitations to everything."

"I don't think it's anything serious. Just a little hobby for the summer. Lynn gets bored when Richard's not around."

"She should be careful, though. Bringing someone like that into the circle. You never know what they're really after. Free drinks, connections, a wealthy husband."

"What could she possibly be after? Look at her. She's not exactly competition."

"Everyone's after something."

Maddie stood frozen. Lynn's little project. Someone like that. These people.

She'd heard enough.

She returned to the living room, her face composed, her decision already made. Lynn was by the windows, talking to

Susie. Kathy was topping off her glass. Everyone carried on—they had no reason not to.

"I'm so sorry," Maddie said, loud enough for the room to hear. "I completely lost track of time. I have a delivery scheduled at the gallery."

Kathy turned. "Oh, that's too bad. We were just getting started."

"Work is work, isn't it?" Maddie smiled, though it was like wearing a mask. "Thank you for having me."

"You'll come back another time," Kathy said. It wasn't a question.

"Of course."

Lynn caught her eye from across the room. Maddie held her gaze for just a moment—long enough to catch a hint of uncertainty—then looked away. She didn't need an explanation. She didn't need Lynn to apologize for bringing her into this world. She just needed to leave.

She made her way toward the door, passing through the kitchen where the catering staff moved between tasks. A woman—the same one who had mistaken her for hired help outside—looked up as she passed. Their eyes met. A look that said *I know exactly what you're feeling right now.*

Maddie gave her a small nod and kept walking.

Outside, the air was different. Lighter. She walked to her car and leaned against it, exhaling slowly. Her hands were shaking, but it wasn't from nerves. It was relief.

* * *

Dominic's was packed when Maddie pushed through the door. The lunch rush was in full swing—every table occupied, a line snaking toward the register, the air thick with the smell of melted cheese and fresh dough. Two guys worked the ovens while a girl at the register called out numbers over the noise.

Dominic was behind the counter, sliding a pie into a box. He looked up as she entered, and his face brightened.

"Hey, you." He handed the box to a waiting customer and wiped his hands on his apron. "Grab a seat by the window—I'll be right there."

She found the one empty chair, a small table tucked in the corner, and watched him say something to the guy at the nearest oven. The guy nodded, and Dominic untied his apron, tossing it on a hook before grabbing two slices and a root beer from the cooler.

"You're busy," she said as he sat down across from her. "You don't have to—"

"They can handle it for ten minutes." He slid the plate toward her. "You look like you need this more than they need me."

The pizza was exactly what she needed—hot, greasy, the cheese stretching in long strings as she pulled the first slice free. Pepperoni and sausage, the edges of the crust just slightly charred. She'd barely touched the mini quiches at Kathy's, and she demolished half a slice before she even looked up.

"So," he said. "What happened?"

Maddie told him everything. How they'd pressured her to sketch them like a performing monkey. How they treated the staff. What she'd overheard—the comments about her work being "street fair" quality, the jokes about her car.

Dominic listened without interrupting, his face shifting through various expressions as the story unfolded. When she finished, he was silent.

"I never liked snobs like that," he said finally. "I've seen those types come through town. The way they look at everything like it's quaint. Like we're all extras in their vacation movie." He shook his head. "You're worth ten of them, Maddie. Your work, your talent, everything about you. Don't let them make you feel small."

"I know." She picked at the crust. "I think what bothers me

most is that I almost believed it. For a minute there, I thought maybe I was lucky to be included. Lucky to be invited into their world."

"Their world isn't better than ours. It's just more expensive."

Maddie smiled for the first time since leaving Kathy's house. "When did you get so philosophical?"

"I've been watching too many nature documentaries. The narrator makes everything sound profound." He nodded toward her empty bottle. "Another?"

"Please."

Through the window, Maddie could see tourists wandering past, couples holding hands, families with kids still sandy from the beach. This was her Ocean City. These were her people. She didn't need crystal champagne flutes and designer furniture to feel like she belonged.

Maddie finished eating and leaned back, the tension finally draining from her shoulders. The pizza shop was still loud around her—orders being called, the register beeping, laughter from a nearby table. It wasn't glamorous. It wasn't impressive. But it was real.

"Thanks for this," she said.

"For what?"

"For listening. For just... being you."

He gathered the empty plates, and they both stood.

"Those people were awful, you know."

She leaned in and kissed him. "I'll call you later."

She was halfway to the door when she glanced down at her wrist. Bare.

Her grandmother's bracelet—she'd left it on the counter in Kathy's bathroom.

"Everything okay?" Dominic called.

"I left my bracelet at Kathy's."

* * *

Nancy hit the stop button on her recording software and sat back, her face aching from trying not to laugh for the past ninety minutes.

"Tell me you got all of that," she said to Joe.

"Every word." Joe was grinning so wide he looked like a different person. "That guy's a natural."

Across the table, Ronnie Lloyd polished off the last of the coffee cake Nancy had set out and brushed crumbs from his hands. He was eighty-one years old, short and broad-shouldered, with a face that had seen everything and eyebrows that moved independently of each other when he got excited.

"That's not even the good stuff," Ronnie said. "I haven't told you about the horse that could count."

"There's more?" Nancy asked.

"Sweetheart, I worked the Atlantic City track for forty-three years. I've got enough stories to fill a whole season of your little show."

Nancy exchanged a glance with Joe. They'd expected a pleasant interview, maybe some colorful anecdotes about the racing scene back in its heyday. What they'd gotten was a masterclass in the art of storytelling, delivered by a man who seemed incapable of telling a boring version of anything.

In that time, Ronnie had told them about a jockey named Danny Fitzgerald who refused to race unless he ate exactly three hard-boiled eggs and touched the left ear of every horse in the stable before a race. "Never missed a day of that routine in twenty-two years," Ronnie had said. "Then one morning in 1978, the cafeteria ran out of eggs. Danny had a meltdown right there in the paddock. Couldn't get on the horse. They had to scratch him from three races." The man never rode professionally again—not because of injury or age, but because he couldn't shake the idea that his luck had run out with those missing eggs.

Then there was the story of a gambler everyone called "Big Marvin" who showed up at the track one summer with a briefcase full of cash and a system he swore was foolproof. "He'd calculated everything," Ronnie had explained, his hands painting pictures in the air. "Speed ratings, track conditions, jockey weights, moon phases—I'm not kidding, moon phases. First week, he's up forty thousand. Second week, up another thirty. People started following him around, copying his bets." By the end of the month, Big Marvin had lost every cent. Then he bet his car on a sure thing and lost that too. Had to buy a bus ticket home. "Taught me something important," he'd added. "The track doesn't care about your system. The track doesn't care about anything."

And Nancy's personal favorite: a horse named Jailbreak who had figured out how to open his stall door with his teeth. "Every night, same thing." Ronnie had laughed. "We'd lock him up, and by morning he'd be wandering the grounds like he owned the place. Found him in the parking lot once, just standing next to a Cadillac, calm as anything. Another time he got into the concession area and ate eleven pounds of peanuts. The vet couldn't believe he was fine." They eventually had to install a special latch that required opposable thumbs. "That horse wasn't fast," Ronnie admitted, "but he was smarter than half the trainers I worked with. And the kicker? He had that name before he ever figured out the latch. Just a coincidence. Or fate, depending on how you look at it."

Ronnie had grown up in Ocean City, started working the stables at the Atlantic City Race Course at eighteen, and spent the next four-plus decades rubbing shoulders with jockeys, trainers, gamblers, and characters of every description. His memory was sharp as glass, and his sense of timing was impeccable.

But that last story—the one Ronnie had teased at the start —Joe wasn't going to let it go.

"The horse that could count," Joe said. "I'm going to need to hear this."

Nancy reached for the laptop. "Hold on—let me get this."

Ronnie waited until she gave him a nod, then leaned forward, eyes bright. "1967. There was this trainer, Carl Casper, worked mostly with second-rate horses, the kind that never won but never quite lost bad enough to be retired. Carl had a side hustle—he'd hang around the bar after races, buying drinks for out-of-towners, telling them he had a gift for reading horses. A sixth sense, he called it. And to prove it, he'd bring them to the stable to meet Clever Charlie, his horse that could do arithmetic."

"Arithmetic," Nancy repeated.

"Simple stuff. Addition, subtraction. Carl would ask him questions and Charlie would tap his hoof the right number of times. Three plus two? Five taps. Eight minus three? Five taps. The horse was never wrong."

"How is that possible?" Nancy asked.

"It wasn't. Not the way Carl was selling it, anyway." Ronnie chuckled. "See, if you can convince a bunch of half-drunk tourists that your horse can do math, it's not hard to persuade them you know which horses are going to win. Carl would take their money, promise to place bets on their behalf with his 'inside knowledge,' and pocket most of it. The ones who won, he paid out just enough to keep them coming back. Classic long con."

"What happened when they found out?" Joe asked.

"Took the track officials three months to figure out he was signaling the horse. Little movements with his hand, so subtle you couldn't see them unless you were looking. Clever Charlie wasn't doing math. He was just really good at reading his trainer. They banned Carl from the track for life." Ronnie held up a finger. "But here's the thing—the horse really was clever. Learned to read Carl's signals so carefully that he could predict when to stop tapping. That's not nothing. That's intelligence. Just not the type Carl was claiming."

Nancy wrote "Clever Charlie" in her notebook, underlining it twice.

"We should probably wrap up," Joe said, checking his watch. "We've been at this for an hour and a half."

"Time flies when you're having fun." Ronnie stood, moving slowly but steadily. "You want more stories, you know where to find me. The diner on West Avenue, every morning at eight. Same booth for the last thirty years."

Nancy walked him to the door, expressing her gratitude three times over. He waved her off with the practiced ease of someone who'd heard it all before.

"Thank you for listening. Most people these days, they don't want to hear from old men about old times. Nice to know someone cares."

After he left, Nancy and Joe sat at the table surrounded by recording equipment and empty plates, both slightly dazed.

"We need to get organized," Nancy said finally. "We've got Jean, Tony, and now Ronnie. That's three solid episodes, maybe four if we split Tony's into parts."

"Plus whatever comes next." Joe pulled out a notepad and pen. "I've been thinking about the release schedule."

"Me too. Summer's really ramping up now. School's letting out, tourists are flooding in. If we're going to launch this thing, the timing's right."

"We should build up a backlog first. At least five or six episodes ready to go before we release anything. That way we've got a cushion."

Nancy nodded, making notes of her own. "Weekly releases? Bi-weekly?"

"Weekly feels right. Keeps the momentum going." Joe clicked his pen. "We should also think about promotion. Getting the word out. Put up flyers at some of the local spots."

"Lauren could help with that. Chipper's and Romano's, for sure."

They talked through logistics for another hour, the conversation ranging from episode length to thumbnail images to whether they should have theme music. By the time they finished, the sun had dropped below the roofline and the room had gone dim.

"This is really happening," Nancy said quietly.

"Seems like it."

"I never thought—" She stopped, suddenly emotional. "Who's going to want to listen to me talk about Ocean City?"

"People want to hear this. They just don't know it yet."

Nancy gathered the gear, handling it with care. Each interview added to the archive, preserved voices that might otherwise fade into silence. Jean and her candy shop. Tony and his decades of secrets. Ronnie and his racetrack full of characters.

There was still so much more to capture. So many people she hadn't talked to yet. So many stories waiting to be told.

CHAPTER NINE

The beach at Ninth Street was already packed by midmorning, towels and umbrellas staking claim to every available patch of sand. Claire had arrived early enough to secure a decent spot near the water, close enough to catch the breeze and watch the waves roll in.

Lauren dropped her beach bag and glanced around. "Not bad at all."

"I've learned a few things since moving here." Claire spread out her towel, anchoring the corners with her sandals and a bottle of sunscreen. "Early bird gets the prime real estate."

"Look at you, becoming a local." Lauren settled onto her own towel, pulling out a paperback she'd already dog-eared halfway through. "I'm impressed."

The June air carried the familiar mix of salt and coconut sunscreen that Claire had come to associate with Ocean City. Around them, families were setting up for the day, kids already racing toward the water despite their parents' calls to wait. A lifeguard whistled from the stand, waving a swimmer back from drifting too far south.

Claire leaned back on her elbows and let the sounds wash over her. This was what she'd imagined when she'd decided to move here. Mornings on the beach with her sister. Bridget and Evan with her on days when they weren't at their dad's, building sandcastles and bodysurfing in the waves. The simple pleasure of having nowhere else to be.

"I have something to tell you," Lauren said, her voice dropping to a near-whisper even though the closest strangers were a good fifteen feet away.

"That sounds ominous."

"It's not ominous. It's just..." Lauren looked over her shoulder. "Keep this between us for now, okay? At least until we have a plan."

"Okay. What's going on?"

Lauren leaned in closer. "Matt and I found something. Recently, when we were kayaking."

"Found what?"

"A cove. Hidden behind the jetty, through a maze of rocks you can only navigate at low tide." Lauren's eyes had taken on a particular gleam that Claire recognized from childhood. "It's covered in sea glass. Not just a few pieces. The entire beach is covered. Layers of it. There's a woman camping there, a freediver named Rae. She's been researching the history. Turns out there was a dump site during Prohibition where bootleggers would toss empty bottles offshore. All that glass has been tumbling in the ocean for a hundred years."

"That's..." Claire searched for the right word. "That's amazing, actually."

"It is. Rae's still documenting everything, and we're trying to figure out what to do next. Once she's further along, we'll probably go public, but for now we're keeping it quiet."

"I won't say anything."

"Thanks. I've just been dying to tell someone. We met Rae the last time we were there—got so caught up talking to her that we missed the tide and ended up stuck overnight. She's been researching it for a couple of weeks. We're heading back tomorrow to see what else she's found."

"I want to see it sometime."

"You will. Once things settle down and Rae's ready. I'll take you."

They fell silent, the quiet that came from decades of shared history. Claire picked up her own book, a thriller she kept meaning to finish but couldn't get past chapter four. The plot kept losing her, her mind wandering to other things whenever she tried to focus.

She was reading the same paragraph yet again when she heard it.

A commotion somewhere down the beach. Voices rising above the general noise, excited rather than alarmed. Claire shaded her eyes with her hand and looked toward the source.

Two men were approaching from the direction of the boardwalk, heading for the water. One was unremarkable, a guy in his thirties with a cooler slung over his shoulder. The other was tall, broad-shouldered, moving with the kind of easy athleticism that drew the eye.

"What's going on?" Lauren sat up, following Claire's gaze.

Before Claire could answer, a teenage boy broke away from his family's umbrella and jogged over to the two men. Then another. A woman abandoned her beach chair and hurried over, phone already raised. Within seconds, a small crowd had formed, people pressing forward, voices overlapping with questions and exclamations.

The tall man laughed and held up his hands in a gesture of good-natured surrender, posing for photos as a kid thrust a phone toward him. His friend stood off to the side, looking amused but unsurprised.

"Is that someone famous?" Lauren asked, craning her neck for a better look.

Claire's breath caught in her throat.

She knew that laugh. She knew the way he ducked his head when he was trying to be modest, the way he scratched the back of his neck when he was slightly uncomfortable. She knew him.

Troy.

"Oh my gosh," she heard herself say.

"What? Do you know him?"

"I've met him. Twice, actually. At the spa, and then at a bar. We talked for hours." Claire watched as Troy accepted another photo request, his smile warm even as more people gathered around him. "I couldn't figure out where I knew him from. He said he got that a lot, but he never told me why."

"Wait." Lauren grabbed Claire's arm, her grip suddenly intense. "Is that Troy Bennett? *The* Troy Bennett?"

"Who?"

Lauren stared at her like she'd grown a second head. "Troy Bennett. The Eagles tight end. He won a Super Bowl like five years ago. He was all over the news when he retired."

Claire felt the pieces clicking into place, the recognition that had been nagging at her finally resolving into something clear. The face she'd seen on magazine covers, on television, on billboards along the highway. Of course she'd known him. Everyone knew him. She just hadn't put it together because she'd been too busy talking to him like a normal person.

"I had no idea," she said weakly.

"How did you not know? He's one of the most famous athletes in Philly. And South Jersey is Eagles country."

"I don't follow football."

"You don't have to follow football. He was everywhere. He did those car commercials."

Claire vaguely remembered the commercials. She had a dim memory of Matt mentioning him once, something about a playoff game. But in her mind, Troy had just been Troy, the guy who couldn't handle a massage and who read books at bars, the guy who'd understood what she meant about starting over.

The crowd around him had grown to maybe twenty people

now, phones and cameras pointing in his direction. Troy was handling it with practiced ease, but Claire could see the slight tension in his shoulders, the way his eyes kept scanning for an escape route.

Then his gaze landed on her.

For a moment, neither of them moved. Then Troy's face broke into a wide grin, and he said something to his friend before making his way toward her.

"I swear I'm not following you," he called out, close enough now that she could hear him over the background noise.

"Could have fooled me." Claire found herself smiling despite her shock. "You seem to turn up everywhere I go."

He stopped a few feet away, looking genuinely pleased to see her. "Third time's the charm, right?"

"Apparently."

Behind him, the crowd was watching with obvious curiosity. A few people were clearly trying to figure out who Claire was, whether she was someone worth paying attention to.

Lauren cleared her throat pointedly.

"Oh." Claire shook herself. "Troy, this is my sister, Lauren. Lauren, this is Troy."

"Nice to meet you." Troy extended his hand, and Lauren shook it with an expression that suggested she was trying very hard to act casual. "Claire's told me about you. You run the breakfast place, right? Chipper's?"

"That's me." Lauren's voice was slightly higher than normal. "Big fan. Really big fan. I watched your whole last season. That game against Dallas was incredible."

"Thanks. That was a good one." Troy's attention drifted back to Claire. "So. Beach day?"

"Trying to, anyway." Claire gestured at the fans gathered behind him. "Though it looks like your beach day might be a little more complicated than mine."

Troy glanced over his shoulder and sighed. "Yeah. This is why I usually stick to the quieter spots. My buddy Levi convinced me to try the main beach for once." He nodded toward the man with the cooler, who was now setting up an umbrella as if nothing unusual was happening. "He's not well known. He doesn't understand."

"Must be rough," Claire said, not entirely hiding her amusement.

"It has its moments." His eyes crinkled. "The worst part is, I really did want to come say hi. Sorry for bringing the circus with me."

"I've seen worse circuses." She nodded toward the onlookers with their phones. "At least this one comes with autographs."

He laughed. "Fair point."

A woman walked up tentatively, teenage daughter in tow. "Excuse me, are you Troy Bennett? I'm so sorry to interrupt, but could we get a picture? My daughter's a huge fan."

Troy's expression shifted seamlessly into his public face, friendly and accommodating. "Of course. Come on over."

He posed for the photo, chatted with the girl about her travel soccer team, signed her beach towel with a marker someone produced from somewhere. Claire watched him navigate the interaction with a kind of professional grace that was clearly second nature.

When the woman and her daughter finally moved on, Troy turned back to Claire with an apologetic look. "Sorry about that."

"Don't be. It's actually kind of fascinating."

"That's one word for it."

"Troy!" Levi called from under the umbrella. "I'm not setting up this whole thing by myself!"

"Duty calls." Troy took a step backward then paused, aware of the people watching them.

Before either of them could say anything else, Matt walked up with sunscreen in one hand. He was still wearing his Jungle Surf T-shirt, clearly on a break from the shop.

"Hey." He handed it to Lauren. "SPF 50 you asked for." Then his eyes landed on Troy. Recognition crossed his face. "You're Troy Bennett."

"Matt, he and Claire have run into each other a few times," Lauren said.

"No kidding." Matt extended his hand, and Troy shook it. "Good to meet you. I watched you play for years. That Super Bowl season was something else."

"Thanks. We had a good run."

"You were a big part of it." Matt said it matter-of-factly, the way he might compliment a well-made surfboard. No gushing, just honest appreciation. "Those car commercials, though. Those were rough."

Troy groaned. "The ones where I had to spike a football through a sunroof?"

"And yell 'That's a touchdown deal!' Fifteen times an hour, all summer long."

"My agent owes me for that one."

They stood there for a moment, the four of them, while the beach carried on around them. A few more people had drifted over, curious, but something about the dynamic kept them from approaching directly.

"Well," Troy said finally, "I should probably go help Levi before he gives up on me entirely." He glanced at the cluster of fans waiting for another chance, then back at Claire. His gaze lingered a beat longer than necessary. "It was good to see you again."

"You too."

He hesitated, like he wanted to say something more, but another fan was already hovering nearby. The moment passed.

He headed off toward his friend, pausing to take a photo with the kid who'd finally worked up the nerve.

"So," Lauren said. "You and Troy Bennett."

"Don't start."

"He seems like a decent guy," Matt said. "Down to earth."

"He is." Claire picked up her book, which she still had no intention of reading.

Lauren and Matt exchanged a look that Claire chose to ignore.

She found herself watching Troy in the distance, still thinking about the way he'd looked at her before he left. Three times now they'd crossed paths. That had to mean something. Or maybe it meant nothing at all. Either way, she hoped it wasn't the last.

* * *

The smell hit Brenna before she even got out of her truck.

She'd been doing this work long enough to know what decomposing jellyfish smelled like, but this was on another level. Thousands of gelatinous bodies covered the sand at Thirty-Fourth Street, baking in the late-morning heat. Moon jellies dominated the scene, their translucent bells catching the light, but scattered among them were the more dangerous specimens: the iridescent blue floats of Portuguese man o' war, the tangled reddish-brown tendrils of lion's mane.

"Every summer I think I've seen it all," Morrison said, joining her at the water's edge. "And every summer this place proves me wrong."

"It's unprecedented," Brenna agreed. "The numbers, the species diversity, the geographic spread. I've been checking with colleagues along the Jersey Shore. They're seeing similar patterns from Cape May to Long Beach Island."

"Any idea what's causing it?"

"Working on it." She pulled out her tablet, scrolling through the latest data. "Water temperatures are elevated, but not by enough to explain this. Salinity's within normal range. I've been looking at satellite imagery of the Gulf Stream. There's an unusual eddy formation about sixty miles offshore. Could be disrupting normal migration patterns."

"How long until we know for sure?"

"Could be days. Could be weeks." Brenna looked out at the shoreline, at the crew picking their way through the mess. "In the meantime, I'll keep collecting samples and monitoring the data."

The cleanup operation was in full swing. Beach tractors rumbled across the work zone, their wide scoops gathering jellyfish into piles that dump trucks hauled away. Volunteers in protective gear worked the areas the machinery couldn't reach.

"Careful with the lion's mane," she called out to a man getting too close to a dark-red cluster. "Their tentacles can still sting even after they're dead."

Morrison stepped away to relay the warning. "You heard her. Use the long-handled nets on those."

The man nodded and adjusted his approach. For a moment, Brenna allowed herself to think they might actually get ahead of this thing.

Then came a sound like a dozen rusty hinges being worked at once, growing louder and more chaotic by the second.

Seagulls. Dozens of them at first, then hundreds, descending on the cleanup site in a shrieking, diving cloud. They'd discovered the jellyfish buffet.

The birds attacked with single-minded fury. They dove at the tractors, pecked at the scooped-up piles before they could be loaded into trucks. Workers ducked and covered their heads, abandoning their posts.

Someone's baseball cap was seized by a dive-bombing gull and carried off like a trophy. Another person tripped over a beach chair, immediately swarmed by birds investigating their cooler. One worker ran for the dunes, arms windmilling, a gull in hot pursuit.

Brenna stood in the middle of it all, watching in horrified amusement as Morrison's carefully coordinated cleanup devolved into pandemonium.

"This is..."

"This is Ocean City," Morrison said beside her, with the weary acceptance of a man who had truly seen everything. "Always something new."

A gull landed on the hood of the nearest tractor, a mangled moon jelly dangling from its beak. It regarded Brenna with what she could only describe as smug satisfaction before taking off again, leaving a trail of jellyfish residue on the machinery.

"City councilwoman at two o'clock," Morrison muttered.

Brenna looked. Sure enough, Councilwoman Kim Stewart was making her way across the sand, heels sinking with every step. She had that particular expression politicians wore when they wanted to be seen showing concern without actually getting their hands dirty.

"Lieutenant Morrison," the councilwoman called out, raising her voice over the commotion. "I wanted to see the progress firsthand. What's the current status of..."

She never finished the question.

A gull, swooping low overhead with something clutched in its talons, released its cargo directly above the councilwoman's head. The half-digested jellyfish landed squarely on her shoulder, splattering across her cream-colored blazer in a spectacle of gelatinous horror.

She froze. Even the seagulls seemed to pause.

Then Kim Stewart let out a shriek that could be heard three blocks away.

"Get it off! Get it OFF!"

Crew members rushed to help with towels and gloves and expressions of barely suppressed laughter.

Morrison sighed. "And somehow it keeps getting stranger."

Brenna couldn't help but laugh. The absurdity of it all, the seagulls and the jellyfish and the shrieking politician, a morning of careful planning undone by a flock of opportunistic birds. Sometimes you just had to surrender to the chaos.

"We'll reconvene at low tide tomorrow," Morrison said,

pulling out his radio. "See if we can get ahead of the birds this time."

"And if we can't?" Brenna asked.

Morrison surveyed the mayhem, the crew retreating to safer ground, the seagulls gorging on their unexpected bounty. The cleanup was only half finished, the tide already starting to turn. Tomorrow they'd be back, and probably the day after that, fighting a battle that nature seemed determined to make as difficult as possible.

"Then we adapt," he said. "That's what we do."

Brenna nodded. She'd stick around, collect her samples, document what she could. That was her job—observe, analyze, try to make sense of it all. The rest was up to Morrison and his team.

The seagulls continued their feast. The councilwoman was being escorted back to her car, designer blazer ruined beyond salvaging. And somewhere in the back of her mind, Brenna was thinking about the satellite data, the Gulf Stream anomaly, the pieces that might finally start coming together.

She kept coming back to those nor'easters last winter, the way they'd churned the coast for weeks. It felt connected somehow, but the timeline still didn't quite add up.

Something was changing out there, beneath the surface. She could feel it. She just didn't know what it was yet.

CHAPTER TEN

Rae handed Lauren the snorkel mask and checked the strap. "Tighten it here. You want it snug but not cutting off circulation."

Lauren adjusted the strap and pressed the mask against her face, creating a seal. The morning was calm, the bay flat as glass, and from the shore of the hidden cove, she could see straight down to the sandy bottom in the shallows.

"We've got maybe two hours before the tide starts turning," Rae said, securing her own mask on top of her head. "Plenty of time to see what's down there."

Matt was already in one of his spring suits—the lighter neoprene he wore this time of year. Lauren had opted for just a rash guard over her swimsuit—the June water was cool but not unbearable. They'd stowed their life jackets in the kayaks for the paddle out. For the snorkeling, Rae had checked that they were comfortable swimmers—the site was calm and protected, easy conditions.

Rae had offered to show them on their last visit, and they'd jumped at the chance. Not the shipwreck—that was too deep for casual snorkeling—but the dump site. The source.

"This isn't just sea glass washing in from somewhere else,"

Rae had told them. "It's coming from right here. A hundred yards offshore, maybe less. And at low tide, you can see it."

Now they stood at the water's edge, the bay stretching out before them. Rae's inflatable sat on the beach, orange and weathered from salt and sun. She dragged it toward the water.

"We'll paddle out past the rocks, then tie off and swim from there. The site's in about four or five feet of water at low tide—easy depth. Probably deeper a century ago, before the sandbars built up. Just stay relaxed, breathe through your snorkel, and don't touch anything sharp."

They pushed off, Rae in the inflatable, Lauren and Matt in their kayaks. The water was clear enough that Lauren could see schools of minnows darting beneath her hull, shadows flashing silver as they moved. A horseshoe crab trundled across the seafloor, prehistoric and unhurried.

They paddled past the rock formations that guarded the cove's entrance, following Rae around a curve in the shoreline. Here the water deepened, the bottom falling away into blue-green murk.

"Just up ahead," Rae called, slowing her inflatable. She guided it toward a cluster of rocks that broke the surface, their tops dark with algae. "We can tie off here and swim from there."

Lauren secured her kayak to a jut of rock and slipped into the water. The cold hit her first then settled into something manageable. She adjusted her mask, fitted the snorkel between her teeth, and ducked her face beneath the surface.

The underwater world opened up before her.

She'd snorkeled before—in the Caribbean, once, on a vacation years ago—but this was different. This was her ocean, the same water that touched the beaches she walked every day, and yet she'd never seen it like this. Shafts of light penetrated the green, illuminating particles that drifted like snow. Below, the bottom rose and fell in gentle ridges, sand giving way to patches of seagrass that swayed in the current.

Matt surfaced beside her, pulling the snorkel from his mouth. "This is incredible."

Rae was already ahead, her fins propelling her toward a darker patch of bottom. She gestured for them to follow.

They swam in a loose formation, Lauren keeping her breathing steady through the snorkel. A flounder burst from the sand beneath her, startling her, and she watched it settle a few yards away, its camouflaged body nearly invisible against the seabed.

Then she saw it.

The sand ahead wasn't uniform. It was mottled, disturbed, and as she drew closer, she began to make out shapes half-buried in the sediment. Bottle necks jutting up at angles. Curved fragments catching what light reached this depth. A corroded piece of metal, maybe a hinge or a bracket, barely visible beneath a layer of silt.

Rae had stopped, hovering above the site, and Lauren pulled up beside her. Through the mask, the dump site spread out in every direction, a graveyard of glass and debris that must have covered a quarter acre. Some pieces were still embedded in the sand, their tops just visible. Others had been exposed by the shifting bottom, their frosted surfaces bright against the murk.

Lauren exhaled slowly, sending a stream of bubbles toward the surface. She'd known this place existed—Rae had told them the theory—but seeing it was something else entirely. A hundred years of bottles, buried and forgotten, now revealed.

She spotted a cobalt bottle still mostly intact, its neck broken but its body preserved. Nearby, a cluster of brown glass —beer bottles, probably—lay scattered like fallen soldiers. And everywhere, the tumbled fragments that eventually washed into the cove, polished and frosted by decades of being churned against sand and stone.

Matt tapped her shoulder and pointed. A skate had appeared at the edge of the site, its flat body barely distinguishable from the sand until it moved, gliding away with a ripple of its wings.

They spent the next hour exploring. Rae led them along the perimeter of the dump site, pointing out features: a section where the bottles were stacked three deep, probably the remains of a crate that had broken apart; a cluster of medicine bottles, their distinctive shapes still recognizable; a single champagne bottle, its heavy base intact, lying on its side like a sleeping giant.

The sea life was abundant. Blue crabs picked their way through the debris. Schools of silversides flashed past, moving as one. Tiny grass shrimp darted between the bottle necks, and a spider crab clung to a piece of corroded metal, its long legs motionless.

When they finally surfaced for the last time, Lauren felt like she'd been somewhere far away, another world entirely.

"That was..." She couldn't find the words.

"I know," Rae said, pulling herself into the inflatable. "First time I saw it, I floated out here for hours. Just trying to process it."

They paddled back to the cove in silence, their minds still underwater. The dump site explained everything—why the sea glass kept coming, why the colors were so varied, why some pieces were impossibly old. An entire history, hidden for generations and suddenly exposed.

* * *

They had lunch on the beach, sitting in a loose circle near Rae's fire pit. Lauren and Matt had packed sandwiches and water bottles in the kayaks. Rae added dried fruit and crackers, some cured meat she'd picked up in town. They ate and let the afternoon stretch out before them.

"So what happens next?" Lauren asked. "With all of this. The dump site, your research."

Rae was quiet for a moment, looking out at the water. "I think I'm ready to publish. Not to a journal—nothing formal. But there are maritime history groups, local preservation societies. People who'd care about this."

"And the location?" Matt asked. "Are you going to tell people where it is?"

"That's trickier." Rae picked up a piece of sea glass from the sand beside her, turning it in her fingers. "Part of me wants to keep it secret forever. But that's not realistic. Someone else will find it eventually. Better it's documented first, understood. Protected, if possible."

Lauren thought about all the glass they'd collected over the past weeks. The bags in her closet, sorted by color. The pieces she'd given to friends. The ones Matt had started selling at the farmers market, testing the waters. "You don't mind that we've been taking some?"

"Taking?" Rae smiled. "You've barely made a dent. And the ocean keeps bringing more. That's the thing about this place—it's not a fixed resource. It's alive. The storms stir things up, new pieces surface, the cycle continues." She gestured toward the water. "There's enough glass down there to last decades. I'm not worried about running out."

They sat with that for a while, the sound of waves filling the silence.

"My mother has a podcast," Lauren said. "About Ocean City. Local history, stories from old-timers. She's always looking for guests."

Rae raised an eyebrow. "A podcast?"

"It's new. She just started recording this summer. Hasn't released anything yet, but she's been gathering stories, collecting memories." Lauren pulled out her phone to check the time. "Let me talk to her. This story—the dump site, the sea glass, the history—it's exactly the kind of thing she's looking for."

Rae considered it. "I've never done anything like that."

"She's good at making people comfortable. And I have a friend who might want to be part of it too—Brenna, she's a coastal ecologist. She's been working with Ocean City on all the jellyfish stuff. Having a scientist and a diver who's done all this research together could make for a great episode."

Rae nodded slowly. "A scientist and a diver. I like it." She started gathering the lunch scraps. "Set it up. I'm in."

* * *

By two o'clock, Nancy's dining room had been transformed into a makeshift studio. Joe had set up extra chairs, tested the microphone levels twice, and arranged a plate of cookies that no one had touched yet.

Rae sat across from Nancy, looking more put together than Lauren had seen her. She'd changed into a simple white shirt and pulled her hair back, though her deeply tanned face and calloused hands still marked her as someone who spent her life outdoors. She studied the microphone setup with the same curiosity she probably brought to a new dive site.

Brenna had arrived ten minutes earlier, after Lauren's call explaining the situation. She'd brought her laptop, loaded with coastal data and satellite imagery, and her eyes had gone wide when Rae started describing what she'd found beneath the water.

"This is remarkable," Brenna had said, scrolling through Rae's photos of the dump site. "You're saying this was completely buried until recently?"

"Entirely. I've been diving this stretch of coast for years. That site didn't exist—or at least, it wasn't visible. Then those storms came through last winter. When I came back this June, everything had changed."

Now they sat together at Nancy's table—Rae, Brenna, and Nancy facing the microphone while Lauren and Matt watched from the kitchen doorway. Joe had the levels dialed in, his laptop open to the recording software.

"Let's start from the beginning," Nancy said, pressing record. "Rae, tell us how you found the cove."

Rae took a breath and began. She talked about the shipwreck she'd been investigating, the *Esther Pearl*, and how a routine dive had led her to something unexpected. She described the maze of rocks, the hidden beach, the carpet of sea glass that seemed impossible until you understood where it came from.

"The dump site dates back to Prohibition, maybe earlier," Rae explained. "Before proper waste disposal, coastal towns just dumped their garbage offshore. Glass bottles, metal cans, broken ceramics. They figured the ocean would take care of it."

"And it did," Nancy said. "In its own way."

"Exactly. The glass got tumbled, polished, turned into something beautiful. The metal rusted away. But the site itself stayed hidden, preserved under layers of sand. Until now."

Brenna leaned forward. "That's where the oceanography comes in. Those nor'easters—they didn't just churn up the surface. They shifted sandbars, redirected currents, changed the entire underwater topography."

"We noticed it with the jellyfish first," Brenna continued. "Species showing up that shouldn't be here, in numbers we've never seen. The water temperatures were elevated. At first I didn't think it was enough to matter, but combined with everything else, the usual patterns weren't holding." She pulled up a chart on her laptop and turned it so Nancy could see. "This is a map of the sandbar formations from last year compared to this year. Look at the difference."

Nancy studied the screen. "That's a dramatic change."

"The storms reshaped everything. And when the seafloor moved, things that had been buried for decades suddenly surfaced." Brenna turned to Rae. "Including a dump site that nobody knew existed."

Rae nodded. "The bottles down there—some of them are still sticking out of the sand at angles. You can see the layers, the way the sediment shifted. It's like the ocean peeled back a century of secrets."

"And that's not all," Brenna said. "That Gulf Stream eddy I've been tracking? It's been pushing warm water closer to shore. The storms, the currents, the water temperatures—it's all connected."

Nancy was scribbling notes, her eyes bright. "So you're saying the same storms caused both of these things? The jelly-fish and the sea glass?"

"The ocean is one system," Brenna said. "When you disrupt it, everything responds."

Brenna paused. She was staring at the charts on her screen, flipping between windows, her brow furrowed.

"What is it?" Lauren asked.

"I've been trying to figure out the timeline. The storms started back in December, then more in January and February, but we didn't start seeing the effects until May, June. There's this lag that didn't make sense to me." She met Rae's eyes. "But if the sediment shift was gradual—if the sand kept moving for weeks afterward—"

"It would," Rae said. "That's how it works. A big storm destabilizes the bottom, but the actual redistribution happens slowly. Like shaking a snow globe. The flakes don't settle right away."

Brenna went still. Lauren watched the pieces click into place behind her eyes.

"That's it," Brenna said. "That's what I've been missing. The nor'easters were the cause, but the effects took months to manifest. The sediment redistributed gradually, the currents adjusted over time, and by the time summer arrived, the whole system had reorganized itself." She sat back, slightly dazed. "The timeline does add up. I just wasn't accounting for the delay."

Nancy had stopped taking notes. "This is incredible. Those nor'easters reshuffled the seafloor, and we're only now seeing the results."

"The jellyfish, the sea glass, probably other things we haven't even noticed yet," Brenna said. "One system, one cause."

They talked for another hour, the conversation weaving between history and science, between what Rae had discovered in her camp and what Brenna had been tracking from her research station. Nancy guided them with questions, drawing out details, making connections none of them had seen on their own.

When they finally wrapped up, Joe announced they'd recorded nearly two hours of material.

"So what do we do with this?" Nancy asked. "We can keep the location vague, or we can tell people exactly where to find it. Your call."

Rae thought about it. "Let's tell them. The location, the history, all of it. A place like that deserves to be shared—it belongs to the community."

Nancy's eyes lit up. "Are you sure? Once it's out there, you can't take it back."

"I'm sure." Rae looked around the table. "I came here to document something special. What's the point if no one ever gets to see it?"

"This could be our first episode," Nancy said, glancing at Joe. "We've been recording all summer, but we haven't released anything yet. This feels like the right one to start with."

Joe nodded. "I can have it edited and ready in a couple days."

"Then let's do it," Rae said.

They said their goodbyes on Nancy's front porch. Rae shook hands with everyone, promised to stay in touch, and mentioned she might head north soon. Cape Cod. Another shipwreck to investigate, this time with friends. Lauren had a feeling they'd see her again.

* * *

The address in Maddie's phone led her back through Avalon and into Stone Harbor, past the familiar turn at the hedge, down the crushed-shell driveway she'd hoped never to see again.

She parked her car near the edge and sat for a moment with her hands on the wheel. She wasn't here to reconnect. She wasn't here to pretend the brunch had been anything other than what it was. She just wanted her grandmother's bracelet back.

The front door opened before she reached it. A young man in a black polo stepped out onto the porch. She recognized him from the brunch.

"Ms. Scott?"

"Yes. I called earlier about—"

"The bracelet. I know. Mrs. Sowers is at tennis, but she left instructions to help you find it." He held the door open. "It's probably still in the bathroom where you left it. If you want to come in and check..."

Maddie hesitated. The last thing she wanted was to walk back into that house, to feel its particular atmosphere pressing down on her again.

"Actually," he said, lowering his voice, "I can just go look. If you'd rather wait out here."

Relief flooded through her. "That would be great. I appreciate it."

He disappeared inside, and Maddie stood on the porch, taking in the manicured grounds. The fountain burbled. A landscaper worked a section of flower bed in the distance. Everything was exactly as it had been before—beautiful, expensive, somehow hollow.

A minute later, the young man reappeared, her grandmother's bracelet in his palm.

"Found it. Right where you said."

Maddie took it, its weight settling into her hand. Such a small thing to have caused so much trouble. "Thank you. Really."

"No problem." He glanced up at the doorframe—a small camera mounted above—then back at her. "Let me walk you to your car."

They crossed the driveway together, shells crunching underfoot. When they were far enough from the house, he spoke again, quieter now.

"Look, I probably shouldn't say anything, but... we all noticed. At the brunch. How you were different."

"Different?"

"You looked at us. Said thank you. Most of the guests here, they don't even see us." He shrugged. "It meant something."

Maddie didn't know what to say. She thought about the server who'd been told to stay out of sight after dropping a glass. All of them invisible until something went wrong.

"Can I ask you something?" she said. "Why do you work here?"

He laughed, but there was no humor in it. "Student loans. This job pays better than anything else I could find. But it's..." He searched for the word. "It's a lot."

"I can imagine."

"No offense, but you probably can't. The hours, the way they talk to you, the—" He stopped himself. "Sorry. I shouldn't be dumping this on you."

"You're not." Maddie reached into her purse and pulled out a twenty. "Here. For going to the trouble of finding this."

He shook his head. "I can't take that."

"You can. For dealing with me showing up unannounced." She pressed it into his hand. "And look—if you ever need a reference, or just want to talk, or know about other job options..." She pulled out one of her gallery cards and wrote her phone number on the back. "There's a pizza place in Ocean City that's hiring. Dominic's, on Asbury. Tell them Maddie sent you. A couple places nearby are looking for people too. And there's a breakfast spot called Chipper's—always needs servers, and the tips are really good. If you're interested in art at all, I could use help at the gallery sometimes. Pays less than this, probably, but the people are decent."

He took the card, studying it. "You don't have to do this."

"I know." Maddie fastened the bracelet around her wrist, the silver cool against her skin. "But you deserve to work somewhere people actually see you."

She got into her car and pulled the door shut. In the rearview mirror, she watched him head back toward the house, the card still in his hand. Behind him, the mansion sat unchanged, its windows reflecting the afternoon sky. But she felt lighter now.

She'd gotten what she came for. And maybe she'd given something too.

CHAPTER ELEVEN

The beach tractors had finished their last pass along the south end of the island, their wide scoops finally empty after days of clearing jellyfish remains. Brenna stood with Lieutenant Morrison at the edge of the work zone as the last crew packed up their equipment. The morning was clear and bright, a perfect day that made tourists forget anything had ever been wrong.

"That's the last of it," Morrison said, pulling off his gloves. "Took us long enough."

"The delay wasn't your fault. Those tractors were tied up with sand replenishment on the north end, and the volunteer coordinators needed time to organize." Brenna checked her tablet, scrolling through the final data. "You handled it well, all things considered."

Morrison let out a breath that seemed to carry the weight of the past week. "Tell that to the councilwoman. She's still finding excuses to avoid me after the seagull incident."

Brenna bit back a smile. The image of Councilwoman Stewart shrieking with jellyfish residue dripping down her blazer had become something of a legend among the beach patrol.

Red flags had been replaced with green along most of the island's beaches. The ocean stretched out before them, deceptively calm, giving no hint of the chaos it had delivered to their shores.

"The podcast should be live soon," Brenna said. "Nancy Romano's releasing it this week. The one about the jellyfish connection to the nor'easters."

"The nor'easter theory?"

"It all fits. The storms shifted the seafloor, disrupted the currents, brought species inland that shouldn't be here." She tucked the tablet under her arm. "We might see similar blooms in future years, but at least now we understand why it happened. That matters."

Morrison nodded slowly. "Knowing why doesn't make the cleanup any easier."

"No. But it helps us prepare for next time."

A lifeguard jogged past, heading toward the newly reopened stretch of beach. Morrison watched him go then turned back to Brenna. "You've been a tremendous help through all this. I know we pulled you away from your research more than once."

"This is my research. Understanding how ecosystems respond to disruption, tracking population shifts, documenting species behavior." She looked out at the water, where a laughing gull circled lazily beyond the breakers. "The jellyfish taught us something. That's always worth the effort."

They shook hands, and Morrison headed toward his patrol vehicle, leaving Brenna alone on the beach. She stayed for a few minutes longer, letting the sound of the waves quiet her mind. The beaches were open. The crisis was resolved. And she had somewhere to be.

* * *

Josh's house sat on a quiet street in Longport, a modest two-story with pale-blue siding and a small front porch. Brenna pulled into the driveway just before ten, her stomach fluttering in a way she refused to acknowledge.

She'd been to his office at the animal hospital. She'd seen him in scrubs, covered in dog hair, wrangling anxious cats and treating wounded terrapins. But this was different. This was his home, his space, the place where he existed when he wasn't being Dr. Grant.

She knocked, and he opened the door almost immediately, like he'd been waiting. He was in jeans and a faded T-shirt, barefoot, and seeing him out of scrubs made her notice things she hadn't before—the breadth of his shoulders, how his eyes brightened when he saw her.

"You found it," he said, stepping back to let her in.

"Your directions were excellent."

The house opened into a living room that felt instantly like him. A sectional sofa faced a fireplace with a mantel crowded with framed photos—Josh in waders, holding a rescued osprey, Josh at what looked like a veterinary school graduation, Josh as a kid on a fishing boat with an older man who shared his jawline. One wall was dominated by a large canvas print of a heron mid-flight, and beside it hung a collection of antique veterinary instruments mounted in a shadow box, their brass and steel dulled with age. Above the fireplace, in a simple wooden frame, was a watercolor portrait of a golden retriever with a graying muzzle and watchful gaze.

A guitar leaned against the wall near the window, and a stack of vinyl records sat on the floor next to a turntable that looked well used. But what really made the space feel lived-in were the cats. A massive orange tabby was draped across the back of the sofa like he owned it. A sleek black cat watched Brenna from the top of a bookshelf, eyes narrowed in judgment. And a third—a gray-and-white tuxedo—wound between Josh's ankles as he led her into the room.

"The grand tour," Josh said, bending to scratch the tuxedo behind the ears. "Living room, obviously. Kitchen's through there. Upstairs is just bedrooms and my office, which is really just where I pile things I don't know what to do with."

"And the welcoming committee?" Brenna asked, already reaching toward the orange tabby.

"That's Mango. He'll let you pet him for approximately three seconds before he bites you. The one judging you from on high is Wednesday. And this guy"—he scooped up the tuxedo—"is Harry. He has no boundaries."

Brenna's gaze drifted to the watercolor above the fireplace. "Who's that?"

A shadow crossed Josh's expression. "Biscuit. She was with me for fourteen years. Lost her last spring." He set Harry down gently. "A client painted that for me. Said a dog like that deserved to be remembered properly."

"She looks like she was a good dog."

"The best." He smiled, the sadness there but not heavy.

"It's nice," Brenna said, looking around the room again. "All of it. It feels like you."

"Is that a compliment?"

"Definitely."

He grinned at that, and she felt like she'd passed some kind of test she hadn't known she was taking.

The kitchen was small but functional, with windows overlooking a backyard that sloped toward a tidal creek. A table had been set for two, and the air smelled like butter and fresh herbs.

"I hope you like omelets," Josh said, moving to the stove. "I'm not a fancy cook, but I can do breakfast."

"I love omelets."

"Good." He cracked eggs into a bowl. "There's coffee if you want some. Mugs are above the pot."

Brenna poured herself a cup and settled into a chair at the table, watching him work. There was an intimacy to it, being in someone's kitchen while they cooked for you, seeing them at ease in a way the outside world rarely allowed. Josh hummed under his breath as he chopped vegetables, a tune she didn't recognize.

"So," she said, "are you going to tell me where we're going after this, or is it still a surprise?"

"Still a surprise." He glanced over his shoulder. "But I think you'll like it."

"Cryptic."

"Mysterious. There's a difference."

"Is there?"

"Cryptic implies I'm being difficult on purpose. Mysterious implies I have a plan." He slid the omelets onto plates and brought them to the table. "I have a plan."

The omelet was perfect, fluffy and filled with peppers, onions, and cheese that melted in her mouth. They ate without hurry, the conversation moving from her work on the jellyfish bloom to his week at the clinic, from childhood memories of the shore to the strange paths that had brought them both here.

"Can I ask you something?" Brenna said, setting down her fork.

"Anything."

"You mentioned your engagement. The one that ended. You said you called it off because something was missing." She hesitated. "What was missing?"

Josh was quiet for a moment, turning his coffee mug in his hands. "Honestly? I'm still figuring that out. She was great— smart, successful, wanted the same things I thought I wanted. But when I tried to picture our future together, it felt like watching a movie about someone who wasn't quite me."

"That sounds lonely."

"It was. And she deserved better than someone who was going through the motions." He looked at her directly. "I didn't want to wake up in ten years and realize I'd built a life with the wrong person. That seemed worse than being alone."

Brenna thought about her own past, the relationship that had faded rather than exploded, two people slowly realizing they had been growing in different directions. "I understand that."

"What about you?" he asked. "What happened with your last relationship?"

"We just wanted different things. He wanted stability, routine, a life where you know exactly what's coming next. I wanted..." She searched for the right words. "I wanted to chase whatever interested me, even if it meant uncertainty. We loved each other, but we couldn't make those two things fit together."

"Do you regret it?"

"Sometimes. Not the ending, but the time it took to get there. We both knew for a while before we admitted it." She picked up her coffee. "But I'm better at being honest with myself now. That counts for a lot."

Josh leaned back in his chair. "For what it's worth, I think the chasing-what-interests-you approach seems to be working out."

"You think so?"

"You're here, aren't you?"

She smiled. "I am."

* * *

They took Josh's car north toward Brigantine, the windows down, the breeze warm against her skin. Brenna had stopped asking about their destination, content to watch the shoreline unfold beside them. Josh kept sneaking glances at her, like he was gauging her reaction, anticipating her response. She caught herself doing the same—her eyes drawn to his hands on the wheel, how relaxed he looked behind it.

When they turned onto Atlantic Brigantine Boulevard and

she saw the sign, she sat up straighter, her whole face brightening.

"The Marine Mammal Stranding Center?"

"You know it?"

"I've heard of it. Never been." She glanced at him. "Josh, this is perfect."

"I hoped you'd think so." He pulled into the small parking lot. "I know someone who works here. She offered to show us around."

The Sea Life Museum was modest from the outside. But when they stepped through the door, Brenna found herself surrounded by the evidence of decades of rescue work. Life-sized replicas of dolphins, seals, and sea turtles filled the space. Display cases held artifacts: vertebrae, skulls, the massive jawbone of a sperm whale mounted on the wall.

"This is amazing," she said, moving closer to examine a dolphin's spinal column laid out in careful sequence.

A woman in a polo shirt with the center's logo appeared from a back room. She was maybe fifty, with calloused hands and a capable presence that came from years in the field.

"Josh! You made it." She smiled and turned to Brenna. "And you must be Brenna. I'm Deb. Josh mentioned you're a coastal ecologist—we could use more people who understand what's happening out there."

Brenna shook her hand. "It's great to finally see this place in person." She nodded toward a poster showing sea turtle rescue protocols. "Do you get many turtles?"

"We had three come through last summer—loggerheads, mostly, and one Kemp's ridley. Boat strikes. Lost one, but the other two made it back out." Deb shook her head. "The plastic's gotten bad too—they mistake bags for jellyfish. By the time they strand, they're often too far gone."

"But not always?"

"Not always. That's why we keep doing the work."

"Deb's being modest," Josh said. "I've seen what they do here. It's impressive."

Deb waved him off. "He's biased. We worked together on a seal case a few years back—fishing line entanglement. The animal pulled through." She gestured toward a large screen mounted on one wall. "Want to see who's here now? The Pool House is off-limits to visitors, but we've got cameras."

The screen showed several enclosures, each containing animals at various stages of recovery. Brenna leaned closer.

"Is that a harp seal?"

"Came in about six weeks ago—malnourished and disoriented. She's healing well." Deb pointed as the image shifted to another enclosure, a sleek gray shape gliding through water. "That's a harbor seal we picked up in April, cold-stunned and underweight. He's put on about ten pounds since he got here. Another few weeks and he'll be back in the ocean."

Brenna watched the seal move through his pool, his movements slightly uneven but purposeful—a small creature fighting his way back to health.

"Thank you for showing us all this," she said to Deb. "What you do here is incredible."

"It's good work," Deb said simply. "That's enough."

They browsed the gift shop before leaving, and Brenna bought a small enamel pin shaped like a sea turtle. Josh tried to pay for it, but she waved him off.

"You planned the whole morning. Let me have this one."

Outside, the salt air hit her face, and she turned to look at him. "This might be the best second date anyone's ever taken me on."

"Only the second date," he said. "Imagine what I'll come up with for the third."

* * *

141

Claire was reorganizing the ribbon display when the bell above Romano's door chimed.

She didn't look up immediately. The ribbons had gotten hopelessly tangled over the past few hours, customers pulling spools out and putting them back in the wrong places. Half the grosgrain was mixed in with the satin, and someone had somehow wedged a roll of burlap into the velvet section. It would take her another twenty minutes to sort it all out.

"I'll be with you in just a minute," she called over her shoulder.

"Take your time."

The voice stopped her cold.

Claire turned, a spool of dusty-rose ribbon still clutched in her hand, and found Troy Bennett standing just inside the door.

He looked different than he had at the beach. More put together, wearing a button-down shirt with the sleeves rolled up and khaki shorts. His hair was neatly combed, and he'd trimmed his beard since she'd last seen him. He looked like someone who had made an effort. His face lit up when he saw her, genuine and unguarded. Like finding her here was exactly what he'd been hoping for.

"Troy," she said. "What are you doing here?"

"Shopping." He said it with complete sincerity, gesturing at the shop around them. "This is a shop, right?"

"Somehow I don't see you as a ribbon guy." She glanced at the spool in her hand then back at him.

"You'd be surprised." He moved deeper into the store, browsing the shelves. His gaze landed on a selection of decorative wreaths. "These are nice. Very... seasonal."

"They're left over from spring."

"Right." He picked up a wreath covered in silk flowers. "This would look great above my fireplace."

Claire couldn't help it. She laughed.

"What?" He looked wounded. "I can't appreciate home décor?"

"I'm just having trouble picturing it."

He set the wreath down and moved to another display, this one featuring vintage tablecloths and napkins.

"Rainbow Brite napkins," he said, reading the label. "Now we're talking."

"Those are from the eighties. Collector's items."

"Perfect. I've been looking for something to class up my dinner parties." He tucked the package under his arm with exaggerated satisfaction.

Claire crossed her arms, watching him with growing amusement. He was terrible at this. Completely, charmingly terrible. And he knew it.

"Troy."

"Yes?"

"Why are you really here?"

He turned to face her, the pretense dropping away. "I remembered you said your family owned a business. Took me a while to figure out which one." He shrugged, a gesture that somehow managed to be both casual and vulnerable. "I thought maybe I could get your number. Since we keep running into each other anyway."

Before Claire could respond, the bell jingled again. A woman in her sixties entered, beach bag in hand, eyes scanning the room.

"Excuse me," the woman said, approaching Claire. "Do you have any shell jewelry? My daughter said you carry some local artists."

"We do. Right over here." Claire led her to a display case on a back wall, pulling out a tray of pendants and earrings. "These are made by a woman in Margate. She does beautiful work with oyster shells and freshwater pearls."

While she helped the customer, Troy wandered through the

store, keeping his distance but staying within earshot. Claire was acutely aware of him, how he moved, how he occasionally picked something up and examined it before setting it back down.

The woman selected a pendant and a pair of earrings, and Claire rang her up. As she was wrapping the purchase, another customer entered, a younger man in a tank top who stopped short just inside the door.

"No way," the man said. "You're Troy Bennett."

Troy's face shifted into something practiced and pleasant. "That's me."

"I can't believe it. My dad's gonna freak out. Can I get a picture?"

"Sure thing."

Claire watched as Troy posed for the photo, patient and gracious despite the interruption. The man thanked him profusely and left without buying anything, phone already raised to share his encounter with the world.

"Can't escape it even in a vintage shop," Claire said once the door had closed.

"Nowhere's safe." Troy made his way back to her. "Part of the territory."

"You're good with people," Claire said.

"Years of practice. Press conferences, fan events, all that." He rested an elbow on the display case. "But it gets tiring. Always being on, always being whoever they expect you to be."

"Is that why you came here? To get away from it?"

"Partly. The shore's always felt different. More anonymous, somehow. People come here to relax, not to hunt for celebrities." He smiled. "Although apparently I can't even buy napkins in peace." He glanced around. "So is this what you do? Run this place?"

Claire laughed. "No, I'm a graphic designer. I just help out at the store when I can. It's my sister's—she runs this and the breakfast spot next door."

"Chipper's," Troy said. "You mentioned it at the bar."

"Good memory."

"I try." His gaze held hers. "I've been thinking about you since Strathmere."

Claire felt her cheeks flush. She busied herself with straightening a row of bookmarks that didn't need straightening. "You're very direct."

"I've learned that life's too short to be otherwise." He shifted the napkins under his arm. "So. Your number. Would that be something you'd be willing to share with a guy who clearly has questionable taste in party supplies?"

"I don't know. Those napkins are pretty concerning."

"I'll grow into them."

She considered him. Troy Bennett, standing in her family's shop, asking for her number like any normal person might. Except he wasn't normal. He was famous and complicated and recently separated.

"I should probably mention," Troy said, as if reading her hesitation, "that I'm going out of town tomorrow. Football clinic in Miami. I'll be gone for about a month."

"A month?"

"Give or take. It's something I committed to months ago. Teaching fundamentals to college prospects, that kind of thing." He leaned against the counter. "But I'll be back. And I'd like to have your number for when I return. You know, in case we stop randomly running into each other."

Claire thought about the past few weeks. Glen with his complaints. Todd with his unsettling research. Two attempts at dating that had left her questioning whether she should bother trying at all.

And then there was Troy. Who showed up unannounced to buy Rainbow Brite napkins. Who talked to her like she was a person, not a project. Who made her laugh in a way she hadn't in longer than she could remember.

"Give me your phone," she said.

Troy handed it over without hesitation. She typed in her number and saved it under her name, then handed it back.

"It's kind of lucky," he said, looking at the screen, "that we kept running into each other. Random chance, three times in a row."

"Actually," Claire said, "it's a little stupid that we never exchanged numbers before. We've had three chances."

"Fair point. I should have asked at the bar."

"You should have."

"I was being respectful. Giving you space."

"You were being slow."

He grinned. "Noted. I'll work on that." He slipped the phone back in his pocket. "So. A month. That's not too long."

"It's not."

"And when I get back, maybe we could get dinner. Something that isn't a spa or a bar or a random encounter at the beach."

"Maybe we could."

The front door opened again, and a group of teenagers tumbled in, chattering about something on their phones. One of them looked up and froze.

"Time to go," Troy said quietly. He set the napkins on the counter and paid quickly, accepting the small bag Claire offered.

He paused at the door, looking back at her one more time. The teenagers were whispering now, phones raised, but Troy seemed to have forgotten they existed.

"See you in a month, Claire."

"See you in a month."

He pushed through the door and disappeared into the afternoon, leaving Claire standing behind the counter with a lightness settling into her chest that she wasn't quite ready to name.

The teenagers crowded around her, buzzing with excitement.

"Was that Troy Bennett?" one of them asked.

Claire turned to the register, keeping her expression neutral. "I really couldn't say."

But she was still smiling when she said it.

147

CHAPTER TWELVE

Nancy had listened to the episode seventeen times.

She'd lost count after midnight, running through it again and again while Joe snored on the couch and the coffee grew cold in her mug. Every cut, every transition, every pause between Brenna's scientific explanations and Rae's descriptions of the cove. It had to be perfect. This wasn't just another story about Ocean City's past. This was happening right now, and it would change everything the moment people heard it.

"You're going to wear out the play button."

Nancy looked up. Morning light was creeping through the blinds, and Joe stood in the doorway, holding two mugs, steam rising from both. She hadn't even noticed him get up from the couch.

"It's done. It's been done for hours."

"I know." Nancy accepted the fresh coffee and took a long sip. "I just keep thinking we missed something."

"We didn't miss anything." Joe settled into the chair beside her, his own mug cradled in both hands. "The audio is clean, the story is solid, and Brenna double-checked all the science. It's ready."

Nancy stared at the waveform on her laptop screen. Two hours of material, edited down to ninety minutes of what she genuinely believed was the best work they'd ever done. Rae's voice describing the glass like it was a living thing. Brenna connecting the dots between the nor'easters and the jellyfish and the sediment shifts that had reshaped the seafloor. Lauren and Matt chiming in about their discovery, that first morning when they'd paddled through the maze and found something impossible waiting on the other side.

"Rae wanted it out there," Nancy said quietly. "She was clear about that."

"She was."

"Once we hit publish, it's gone. We can't take it back."

Joe set down his coffee. "That's true of everything worth doing."

Nancy looked at him—really looked—and saw the same mix of excitement and fear she'd been wrestling with all night. They'd been building toward this all summer, and now it was finally happening. Jean, Tony, Ronnie, now Brenna and Rae. A handful of interviews that somehow felt like a lifetime's worth of stories. But this was different. This was the moment they stopped preparing and started actually doing.

She reached for the mouse.

"Together?" she asked.

Joe put his hand over hers.

They clicked.

* * *

The notification chimed on Lauren's phone at 6:47 a.m., just as she was sliding the first tray of muffins into the oven at Chipper's.

New episode from Shore Stories: "The Hidden Cove—Ocean City's Secret Sea Glass Beach"

Her heart stuttered. She wiped her hands on her apron and tapped the link, scrolling through the episode description. There it was, in black and white. The location. The directions. The story of how a coastal ecologist, a shipwreck diver, and a couple of local business owners had stumbled onto something extraordinary.

Bobby glanced up from the grill. "Everything okay?"

"Yeah." Lauren slipped the phone back into her pocket. "Yeah, everything's fine."

But her mind was already racing ahead. Nancy had warned her this was coming, had given her a heads-up about the timing. Still, seeing it live felt different. Real in a way it hadn't before.

She pulled out her phone again and texted Matt.

It's out.

His response came thirty seconds later: *Saw it. Jungle Surf's going to need more kayak rentals.*

Lauren laughed despite herself. Leave it to Matt to think about business first. But beneath the joke, she knew what he really meant. Their quiet cove, their secret place, was about to become everyone's destination.

She hoped Rae had been right. She hoped there really was enough for everyone.

* * *

By noon, Nancy's phone had become a small rectangular emergency.

"Twelve voicemails," she said, scrolling through the list. "Three interview requests. Someone from the *Philadelphia Inquirer* wants to do a feature."

Joe was hunched over his laptop, refreshing the analytics dashboard every few minutes like it was some kind of nervous tic. "We just passed eight thousand."

"Eight thousand plays?"

"In five hours." He looked up, slightly dazed. "Nancy, most new podcasts are lucky to get a hundred on their first episode."

The reactions were pouring in too. Social media posts, emails. People sharing memories of sea glass hunting with their grandparents. Questions about the best time to visit. A few skeptics demanding proof that the cove was real. And underneath it all, a growing buzz of excitement that Nancy could feel even through the cold remove of the internet.

Her phone rang again. She didn't recognize the number, but when she answered, it was another interview request—a blogger who covered South Jersey tourism. She took down his information and promised to call back.

"This is really happening," she said after she hung up.

"Told you," Joe said. "People want to hear these stories. They just didn't know it until someone started telling them."

* * *

Brenna got the call from Morrison at two o'clock.

"You need to see this," he said. "South end of the island, near the jetty. Bring binoculars if you have them."

She drove down with the windows open, the salt air rushing through the cab of her truck. Even before she reached the beach access, she could see something was wrong. Or right. Or whatever word you used for controlled chaos that seemed to be unfolding exactly as everyone had planned.

Cars lined both sides of Tennessee Avenue, parked bumper to bumper all the way back to the traffic circle. Beach Patrol trucks were positioned at intersections, officers directing traffic with the kind of resigned patience that suggested they'd given up trying to fight the tide. Families streamed past on foot, hauling every kind of watercraft imaginable, their excitement palpable even from a distance.

She found Morrison at the boat ramp, clipboard in hand, surveying the parade.

151

"How bad is it?" she asked.

"Depends on your definition." He gestured toward the water. "Take a look."

The channel leading to the cove was visible from here, a narrow gap between the rocks. Except now it was crammed with boats. Kayaks of every color formed a slow-moving train through the entrance. Paddleboarders wobbled alongside them, some more successfully than others. A family in matching life jackets navigated an inflatable raft that looked barely seaworthy, their children shrieking with delight as they bumped against the boulders.

"They're bottlenecking at the entrance," Morrison said. "Current's fighting them going in, but people are being patient. For now. Luckily the tide's in our favor today—should stay passable until seven or so."

"Anyone hurt?"

"Couple scraped knees. One kid got a paddle to the face, but he's fine—more embarrassed than anything." Morrison almost smiled. "My guys have been great. Blake set up an informal traffic pattern, keeping the inbound and outbound streams separate. Thompson's stationed at the mouth of the channel, making sure no one tries anything stupid."

Brenna watched a woman on a paddleboard lose her balance and pitch sideways into the water. Before anyone could react, two kids in a tandem kayak maneuvered over and helped her climb back on, steadying her board until she found her footing again.

"Strangers helping strangers," she said.

"Saw that happen three times already." Morrison's expression was hard to read. "It's strange. I expected chaos—people pushing, arguments over right-of-way. Instead they're just... cooperating."

Above them, the distant thrum of helicopter rotors cut through the afternoon air. Brenna shaded her eyes and looked up. A news chopper was circling the jetty, its camera probably capturing footage that would be on every evening broadcast from here to New York.

"The station has a boat," she said. "Research vessel. It's small, but there's room for five or six. I was thinking of anchoring outside the channel, getting a better view."

Morrison raised an eyebrow. "You offering to take passengers?"

"If Beach Patrol can spare anyone who wants to watch history happen."

"I might take you up on that." He checked his radio. "Let me make sure things are stable here first."

* * *

The Spartina wasn't much to look at—a twenty-four-foot research vessel with peeling paint and an engine that coughed before it caught—but she'd served the research station well for years. The deck was cluttered with sampling equipment, most of it pushed aside now to make room for passengers.

Matt and Lauren were the first to arrive, bearing a cooler that turned out to contain sandwiches, drinks, and a bag of salt-and-vinegar chips that Matt claimed were essential for any proper boat outing.

"Couldn't miss this," Lauren said, settling onto a bench along the side. "After everything, I need to see it with my own eyes."

Claire showed up next, looking slightly uncertain. "I've never been on a research boat before. Do I need to do anything?"

"Just don't fall overboard," Brenna said. "And if you do, aim for the stern—the propeller's at the back."

Claire's expression suggested she wasn't sure if that was a joke.

Morrison arrived last, still in uniform, his radio crackling periodically with updates from his team onshore. He'd brought

Thompson with him, a young officer Brenna had worked with during the jellyfish cleanup. Both of them looked like they could use a break.

"Blake's got things under control," Morrison reported. "Told him to call if anything changes."

Brenna fired up the engine—three tries before it caught—and eased the Spartina away from the dock. The channel was on the east side of the jetty, maybe a quarter mile from the marina. As they motored around the rocks, the full scope of the situation revealed itself.

"It's even crazier from out here," Thompson said.

The waters around the cove entrance resembled the starting line of a very disorganized regatta. Dozens of kayaks. Paddleboards of every size. Inflatable rafts, one of which appeared to be shaped like a giant flamingo. A few brave souls on boogie boards, using their arms to paddle toward the rocks.

"There must be a hundred people out here," Lauren said.

"More inside the cove, probably." Matt was standing at the rail, binoculars pressed to his face. "I can see the beach through the opening. It's packed."

Brenna anchored the Spartina about fifty yards from the channel entrance, close enough to watch but far enough to stay clear of the traffic. From here, they had a perfect view of the procession.

Lauren opened the cooler and started passing out sandwiches. "I didn't know how many people were coming," she said. "We might have overpacked."

"No such thing," Morrison said, accepting one.

Through the channel entrance, they could catch glimpses of the cove itself—figures moving on the beach, the glint of glass in the sun.

"She's going to fall in," Thompson predicted, watching a little girl lean precariously over the edge of a kayak to grab something from the water.

"Nah," Morrison said. "Kids are sturdier than they look."

"What do you think they'll find in there?" Claire asked.

Brenna thought about everything Rae had said during the recording. The endless carpet of glass. The way the colors shifted depending on the light. The strange, almost magical quality of a place that had existed undiscovered for who knew how long.

"More than they expect," she said.

* * *

By late afternoon, the Spartina had become a floating observation post.

They'd gone through most of the sandwiches and all of the chips. Claire had discovered the sampling equipment and was asking questions about water quality testing that Brenna was happy to answer. Morrison and Thompson had removed their uniform hats, the first sign of relaxation either of them had shown all day.

Morrison's radio buzzed with an update from the shore. No incidents, no arguments over territory. Just people sharing a beach that had enough treasure for everyone.

Matt was eyeing the two-person kayaks strapped to the Spartina's stern—Brenna kept them on board for field sampling in shallow areas. "Any chance we could borrow one of those?"

Brenna was already reaching for the straps. "I was thinking the same thing. After hearing so much about this place, I should finally see it."

They lowered both two-person kayaks into the water. Matt and Lauren took one; Brenna and Claire took the other.

"You good here?" she asked Morrison.

"Go." He waved them off. "Thompson and I can hold down the fort."

Brenna pushed off from the Spartina and fell into rhythm behind Matt and Lauren. The channel entrance was less congested now, the early rush having given way to a steadier trickle of visitors. She followed them in, ducking under a low overhang as Lauren and Matt guided them through the twists.

When they emerged into the cove, she stopped paddling and let the kayak drift.

It was everything she'd expected and nothing like she'd imagined. The beach shimmered with sea glass, layers of color catching the afternoon sun—more than she'd believed possible even after everything she'd heard. And scattered across this impossible carpet: families, children running back and forth with fistfuls of glass, couples sitting together sorting through their finds. A group of teenagers had turned it into a competition, racing to see who could find the rarest colors.

But what struck her most was the sound. Laughter. Conversation. The excited shouts of discovery layered over the steady rhythm of the waves. This place that had been silent and secret for so long was alive now, filled with voices.

They beached the kayaks and waded ashore. Matt and Lauren immediately started picking through the glass, unable to help themselves. Brenna walked the perimeter instead, taking it all in.

A little boy tugged on his mother's arm, holding up a piece of green glass like it was an emerald. An older man sat near the driftwood, sketching the scene in a small notebook.

This was what Rae had wanted. What they'd all wanted, even if they hadn't known it at first. The cove wasn't diminished by being shared. If anything, it felt richer.

They stayed for nearly an hour before paddling back to the Spartina.

Lauren climbed up onto the deck first, sand stuck to her legs, already digging through the pockets of her shorts. She pulled out piece after piece of sea glass. Green, amber, white, another blue. "I kept telling myself to stop picking them up. But they're everywhere. You can't help it."

She held up a small red piece, no bigger than her thumb-nail, but vivid as a ruby in the warm light.

* * *

The sun was dropping toward the mainland when Morrison finally decided it was time to head in. The crowds had begun to thin—families packing up, heading back to shore.

Brenna eased the Spartina away from her anchor point and motored slowly past the rocky passage. From here, she could see all the way to the cove's beach, could make out the tiny figures still moving across the sand, still bending to pick up treasures, still filling their pockets and their bags and their hearts with something they'd never known they were looking for.

Claire leaned against the rail, watching the last of the kayakers navigate their way out of the rocks. "Do you think it'll be like this every day now? This many people?"

"For a while, probably." Brenna guided the Spartina around the jetty's edge. "Eventually it'll settle down. Become part of the routine. People will talk about the first summer, the way they talk about any big event. But the glass will keep washing up. The cove will keep being there. Some things don't run out."

Matt had his arm around Lauren. It had been a long day, chaotic and exhilarating, utterly unlike anything she could have anticipated that morning when she'd slid the first tray of muffins into the oven.

The Spartina rounded the final stretch of rocks, and the marina came into view. Lauren was still holding that red piece of glass, turning it over in her fingers, watching it catch the last of the daylight.

"I'm keeping this one," she said. "Not to sell, not to display. Just to remember."

"Remember what?" Claire asked.

Lauren looked back toward the jetty, toward the hidden cove that was already disappearing from view, toward the place where an entire town had gathered to share something extraordinary.

"That some secrets," she said, "are better when they're told."

EPILOGUE

The calendar on Lauren's kitchen wall was filling up with summer plans, but one date stood out: July 26th. She circled it twice with a red marker.

"You're sure your place has a better view?" Matt asked, leaning against the counter. "Mine has that corner angle."

"You don't have the deck space." Lauren capped the marker and dropped it into the junk drawer. "Trust me. We'll be able to fit everyone and still have a clear view when the boats come by."

Night in Venice. She remembered watching the parade as a kid, sitting on a dock at her grandparents' friends' house with a cup of lemonade and a bag of pretzels, waving at the passengers as they drifted by. It was one of those Ocean City traditions that never got old, no matter how many years had passed between viewings.

"I'm thinking we invite everyone," Matt said. "Friends, family, the neighbors. Make it a real thing."

"We can fit more people on the dock too," Lauren said. "Everyone loves sitting with their feet dangling off the side."

"What time should we tell people to come?"

Lauren thought about it. "The parade starts at six-thirty,

but the boats won't reach this part of the bay until later. Maybe five? That gives people time to settle in before things get going."

"And parking," Matt said. "We should let everyone know to get here early. The streets fill up fast."

"Good point. We can fit a few cars in my driveway, and maybe Erin and John will let us use theirs since they'll be out on their boat."

Through the kitchen window, Lauren could see the boat tied up at their neighbors' dock. Erin had mentioned that John decorated it every year, each theme more elaborate than the last. Lauren wondered what he had planned this time.

Matt straightened up and walked over to the window, standing beside her. The bay stretched out in front of them, blue-gray and calm in the late afternoon. A few boats were motoring toward the marina or out toward the inlet.

A heron was perched on a nearby piling. In a month, this section of water would be lit up with lights and the sounds of crowds cheering. Lauren could picture it.

But she was also wondering what the rest of the summer might hold.

* * *

Pick up book 7 in the Ocean City Tides Series, **Ocean City Sea Foam,** to follow Lauren, Matt, and the rest of the bunch.

Have you read the Cape May Series? If not, start with book 1, **The Cape May Garden**.

Coming soon! A **Sea Isle City** series.

ABOUT THE AUTHOR

Claudia Vance is a writer of Women's Fiction and Clean Romance. She writes feel good reads that take you to places you'd like visit with characters you'd want to get to know.

She lives with her boyfriend and 2 cats in a charming small town in New Jersey, not too far from the beautiful beach town of Cape May. She worked on television shows and film sets for many years. She's an avid gardener and nature lover.